14 Fictional Positions

Short Fictions

by

Eric Miles Williamson

Published by Raw Dog Screaming Press
Bowie, MD

First Edition

Book design: Jennifer Barnes

Printed in the United States of America

ISBN: 978-1-933293-97-4

Library of Congress Control Number: 2010928479

www.RawDogScreaming.com

WHAT PEOPLE WROTE about *East Bay Grease*:

"Williamson's writing becomes transcendent. His prose cuts loose in torrid rhythms that evoke the peril and exuberance of jazz."—*The New York Times Book Review*

"Le livre d'Eric Miles Williamson n'est pas un polar, malgré les morts violentes qui le parsèment, mais un splendide roman noir. Ce premier roman possèune force extraordinaire."—*Paris Match*

"*East Bay Grease* has its own brand of originality. A confident debut, and an arresting, often harrowing read."—*The London Times*

"A foster son of old Jack London—in every best sense—Eric Williamson gives us not only the sorrow and the pity of a tough Oakland life, but—stand back—a lyrical reminder that white trumpet players are people too."—*Barry Hannah*

about *Two-Up*:

"Reading Eric Miles Williamson's new novel, *Two-Up*, is a little like falling face-first against a concrete slab. It puts you in close touch with cold reality and could even change you forever."—*The San Francisco Chronicle Book Review*

"Some novelists enter readers' brains subtly. Not Eric Miles Williamson. He enters noisily, with a jackhammer. Williamson, the bard of the blue-collar laborer."
—*The Kansas City Star*

"*Two-Up* is a rare work of fiction whose sharp realism and dark center recall the sagas of an earlier, more authentic sort. Williamson's triumph is to open up one of the great currents of American literature, the saga of the American worker, a bloody, battered, disabused hero. *Two-Up* is an effort where words never fail."
—*The Bloomsbury Review*

about *Oakland, Jack London, and Me*:

"It's not just because both writers are from the slums of Oakland, California, that Williamson is such a passionate advocate for London. His white-hot scorn for literary fashion lights up nearly every sentence here. One of the least politically correct texts of our time."—*The Atlantic Monthly*

"Williamson is right in thinking he's the perfect person to assess London's worth. He has brought one of America's great writers more alive for all."
—*Milwaukee Journal Sentinel*

"Fans of *White Fang* and *The Iron Heel* will rejoice. The deconstructionists, on the other hand...As if Norman Mailer had devoured Derrida and spit out the bones."—*Kirkus Reviews*

"Williamson is most effective in blasting the pretentious, theory-ridden, politically (if not ethically) correct academic Establishment. And his aim hits the target dead center in a tough but honest, often brilliant indictment of current literary critics with their supercilious and jargonish posturing."—Earle Labor, editor of *The Portable Jack London*

and about *Welcome to Oakland*:

"This powerful slice of greasy, grimy life is highly recommended."—*Library Journal*

"Eric Miles Williamson is the mystic on the street corner."—*East Bay Literary Examiner*

"Most readers will veer away from Eric Miles Williamson's *Welcome to Oakland* the way they would from a street gang descending on their car with tire irons and handguns...Williamson gives a contemporary turn on a literary genre pioneered by Hugo, Dostoyevsky and Céline, and in the American canon by Kerouac, Burroughs and Bukowski....Ignoring Williamson would be a mistake."—*The Washington Post*

"*Welcome to Oakland* is an avalanche. Has the energy of Henry Miller. As Nin used to call me the next Henry, I pass the baton to Eric Miles Williamson."—*Ronald Sukenick*

For my professors, living and dead:

N.V.M. Gonzalez, Robert Williams, Jake Fuchs, Robert Neely, Ronald Sukenick, Steve Katz, Edward Dorn, Anselm Hollo, Robert Phillips, Harmon Boertein, George Trail, Richard Howard, James Tuttleton, Harold Bloom, Denis Donoghue, Jacques Derrida, and Donald Barthelme.

Were it not for them, I'd still be a construction worker, and my books would not exist. Maybe I wouldn't, either.

Also by Eric Miles Williamson

Novels

East Bay Grease
Two-Up
Welcome to Oakland

Nonfiction / Criticism

Oakland, Jack London, and Me

Acknowledgements

Stories in this collection have appeared, in various postures and attitudes, in the following magazines, journals, and newspapers:

The Arkansas Review
Buffalo Press
Continental Drifter
Eat it Alive
Gulf Coast
i.e. magazine
The Iowa Review
The Kansas City Star
Literal Latté
Moral Kiosk
The Slate
The Texas Review
The Yalobusha Review

Many thanks to the editors of these publications.

14 Fictional Positions

Positions

Preface: A Fictional Position

The development and rise of the American short story in the 19th century was the result of simple market forces. Because urban populations in America were so unstable, workers moving from city to city as new lands and employment opportunities arose, newspapers found that serializing novels was bad business: advertisement space was worthless alongside a chapter from a novel that no one lived in town long enough to read. British novelists like Dickens and Trollope published their novels first in serial form, and then collected the chapters together to sell as a book. American novelists had very few venues for serialization, which is why the shape of the American literary novel differs so radically from its British counterpart: chapters from serialized novels read like episodes of soap operas—each chapter opens with a crisis that is soon resolved and closes with the introduction of a new crisis or cliffhanger which will be resolved at the beginning of the next installment. Not so with the American novel—think *Moby Dick* or *Huckleberry Finn*.

With no periodical market for the novel in the U.S., writers of fiction in the first half of the 19th century borrowed the form of the short tale from German authors such as Wilhelm Kleist and E.T.A. Hoffmann and altered the form to suit American newspapers. The result was the literary form we now know as the short story.

What we now know as a literary form, however, was originally no more high Art than is pop music today. Short stories were commercial products written for newspapers and magazines by writers who were trying to make a living at it. Poe tried to elevate the short story to the condition of Art, and Hawthorne produced a few volumes; there's Melville's *Piazza Tales*, and the little busybody Washington Irving wrote *The Knickerbocker Tales*. For the most part, however, the short story was a mere short entertainment akin to a sit-com or hour-long drama on the television.

By the time William Dean Howells took over the editorship of *The Atlantic Monthly* in 1871 the short story form had split into two distinct categories, the same way other art forms split into that which aspires to the Condition of Art and that which exists only to make money. The literary short story had become an art form, but it was also an art form which paid *real* money. For instance, Jack London once had a contract with *Cosmopolitan* to write a story a month for a year at the rate of $1000 per story. I once did the math on this number, using rents in Oakland, California as the index of the value of the dollar, and that thousand dollars a hundred years ago is worth about $250,000 in today's money, what one would get for selling film rights to Hollywood. When a novelist at the turn of the 20th century needed cash to support the novel-in-progress, he would write a short story, and the money would sustain him nicely for a good long while. And it's no surprise that the short stories, written for money as they most often were, were generally not of the same caliber or difficulty as the novels produced by the same authors. Compare the difficulty level differences between the stories and novels of Henry James and William Faulkner and this becomes obvious.

The rise of film, however, changed the status and ultimately the function of the short story permanently. Just as photography negated the mimetic function of the art of painting, rendering the imitative function of painting obsolete, film's rise obliterated the short story's function of delivering short narratives. This took some time, as not everyone had a movie theater nearby and open all hours of the day and night, but today, with movies available with the click of a mouse or remote control, obtaining a short narrative that not only tells a story but which *shows* the story as well, the short story, for the greater public, has become an artifact of the past and curiosity of the present.

When photography disrupted the mimetic function of painting, artists responded by making paintings that were decidedly non-mimetic, that used as a premise the notion that what they were painting was not *reality*, but an artist's *impression* of reality. Monet's Cathedral of Notre Dame paintings are not attempts to realistically render the church any more than Van Gogh's "Starry Night" is an attempt at astronomical accuracy.

The short story has followed suit. When its narrative function was usurped by film, short story writers focused increasingly on the other aspects of the art of fiction. Robert Coover attempts to obliterate narrative certitude, Donald Barthelme operates like a collagist and pop-culture analyst, John Barth fuses criticism, mythology and narrative, the minimalists favor style over substance, and it's almost a universal law that whatever conflict is introduced *is not* going to be resolved (in rebellion to film, which almost always resolves conflicts neatly and with divine finality). The short story has responded to film by attempting to render in fiction that which is *unfilmable*.

The short story has evolved into a different creature than its forbears. The short story is no longer a popular narrative medium. Like poetry, the short story has honed itself out of the public eye and entered the depopulate badlands of Art.

There are very few commercial venues in the country for the short story—*Harper's, The Atlantic, Playboy, The New Yorker, Esquire* and perhaps a few others. Short story writers publish in literary journals for nominal pay—a few hundred dollars at best—or, as is usually the case, no pay. The majority of readers of short stories are the short story writers themselves—mirroring the state of contemporary poetry. Operating beneath the radar of any culture but their own, short story writers are creating works of Art that bear little semblance to the works being created by novelists. Uncompensated (except perhaps with university posts), unread, short story writers, like poets, are free to write whatever they want to write without fear of low sales, public censure, or even bad book reviews, since their collections, published primarily on university and small presses, usually don't get reviewed in anything other than the journals in which the stories originally appeared.

Ask the editors of most literary journals: there are probably more "*writers*" of short stories than there are *readers* of them, far more submissions than subscribers, all those would-be writers scrambling around trying to get published in literary quarterlies no one reads (often not even the would-be-writer submitters!) except other short story writers and poets. Journals get hundreds of thousands of short story submissions every year, but a short story collection is lucky if it sells even a thousand copies. Short story collections tend to be consigned to the oblivion of small press purgatory, where, without publicity budgets, media coverage, or often even distribution, the books become curiosities for the literary historians of the future even before they exist in print.

My point, finally, is this: the American Short Story has its own unique history and pattern of development. This history and development *is not* the same as that of the American Novel, which is still a thriving medium and a medium with a wide range of aesthetic intent. The American Short Story, as a popular form, is extinct. Its descendant, the Short Story as Art Form, survives, albeit in the literary fringes of the culture.

In America the novel is generally (although not overtly) favored, granted more prestige, than the short story.

The American Short Story may be fiction, but it is not the same type of fiction as the American Novel.

The Short Story may garner less prestige, but it is nonetheless as worthy an art form as the Novel.

When I was a college freshman—a music major—I took a beginning course in fiction writing, figuring it would be an easy A, a blow-off. We were required to write short stories. I'd never before read one, blue-collar music nerd that I was, fresh off the construction site and from the Mexican nightclubs in which I played *cumbias* and *rancheras* and *salsa* and *merengue*.

I wrote two stories that semester—one about my messed-up family and the Hell's Angels who reared me, the other about the construction work I'd done before entering college. Both stories got published pretty quickly in national journals—*Smackwarm* (now the *Nebraska Review*) and *The California Quarterly*. The one that got published in *Smackwarm* was so poorly written, so larded with my youthful and unlearned ignorance, so thoroughly rotten that many years later, when driving across the country, I stopped at every university library I could, and if I found the issue that contained my awful story, I tore the pages out and shredded them, throwing the paper ribbons into a trash can in the men's room, where they belonged. The only saving grace concerning my early stories is that they served as prototypes for what would eventually become my novels, *East Bay Grease*, *Two-Up*, and *Welcome to Oakland*.

During the 30 years it took me to write those novels I periodically returned to the form of the short story. Not because I enjoyed writing them—because I didn't and still don't—they're far too difficult for me to write, and I tend to be longwinded anyway—but to try out tricks and gimmicks I was appropriating from my betters, literary innovations perfected by the great living and dead masters. I'll not venture proposing that the stories which constitute *14 Fictional Positions* are nothing more than exercises, but in many ways that's the function they've served for me. By writing short stories I'm practicing linguistic and formal techniques I employ when writing novels. So by definition these stories are apprentice work, this novelist's training ground.

The earliest of the stories collected here date from 1984-1986, when I was a graduate student at the University of Colorado, where I studied with Fiction Collective authors such as Ronald Sukenick, Clarence Major, Robert Steiner, and Steve Katz. Across town, at Naropa, was Allen Ginsberg, who I'd see at the supermarket on occasion. Fridays the Black Mountain poet Ed Dorn bought me beers at the Boulderado Hotel. The rule of the day was to experiment and innovate, to stretch the language to its breaking point and to invent appropriate forms to contain the language. Hence the coyness and silliness of stories like "The Professor Asks His Students if They Agree With the Conclusion: The Table Is an Imitation and Therefore Not Real," "Wamsutter in Dali Vision" (written after reading Walter Abish), "H A N G M A N" and "Third Person on a Bed Built for Five." I look back at them now and I blush remembering the giddiness of the young man—then only 23 years old—who wrote these little ditties. That guy, young Mr. Williamson, he'd only been reading novels and short stories for two years, and yet not only did he presume to have the technical facility to write stories, but he had the nerve to send them to magazines for publication. Young Mr. Williamson believed at the time he was doing new things with form and content, with linguistic and semantic construction. Young Mr. Williamson hadn't yet even read James Joyce, let alone T.S. Eliot or Gertrude Stein.

I continued writing short stories at the University of Houston, where I studied with Donald Barthelme until his death in 1989. There I began

work in earnest on the two books which would become *East Bay Grease*
and *Two-Up*. Novels don't do so well in creative writing workshops, and
so I'd write short stories as required for class while continuing work on
my novels under a cloak of secrecy. The stories I produced during my
eleven years in Houston all served to help develop my novelistic chops.
"A Wise Man is Known by His Laughter," the title swiped from John
Donne and tweaked a bit, was written in 1986 in a single sitting, an all
night caffeine and nicotine and whiskey burst of jubilance at being once
again in a major city (I grew up in the San Francisco Bay Area). The
exuberance and urgency I thought I was expressing grew into the voice of
my most recent novel, *Welcome to Oakland*. Other stories written during
my Houston years include "The Cow Island Open" (a Robert Coover
rip-off), "Mr. Murphy's Wedding," "Creusa" (a Hemingway homage of
sorts), "Phrases and Philosophies for the Use of the Young" (the title and
method swiped from Oscar Wilde), "Kickshaws" (toying with writing
only dialogue á la Manuel Puig), "Rhoda's Sack" (written after reading
Robert Coover's little novel, *Spanking the Maid*) and "Hope, Among Other
Vices and Virtues" (an homage to a man who later appears as a character
in *Welcome to Oakland*). All these stories were written under the immense
and looming presence of Donald Barthelme, who haunts me to this day.
It's as if he stands behind me as I write, grimacing in disapproval, shaking
his head slowly and saying, "No. That will not do, young Mr. Williamson.
That will not do." The final story of this collection is, of course, a playful
tribute to Mr. Barthelme, originally written on cocktail napkins at Old
Barney's, my watering hole of choice in Warrensburg, Missouri, hours
before I was to read a ghost story at a bar. I hope his austere and saintly
ghost will not be offended.

   It was Donald Barthelme who convinced me to abandon imitating
postmodern authors (as I'd been doing) and pursue my own brand of
realism—what I've called in print "Meta-Realism"—a kind of realism

informed by modernism and postmodernism, utilizing innovations and techniques of the experimenters, all the while presenting something that resembles mimesis.

And so *14 Fictional Positions*: Readers of my novels and even my literary criticism and reviews may find this book entirely out of character—a far cry from the urban realism they have likely come to expect of my work—a strange set of oddities and curiosities, a doggie-bag of conceits. This, of course, would be no surprise for its author. To me, though, there's nothing in this collection that doesn't directly relate to my corpus of prose. Realism, or, if you will, "Meta-Realism," would never advance, never develop or improve were it not for the oddities among its precursors. Dostoievsky's Underground Man makes possible Henry Miller, Hardy's muscular prose makes possible D.H. Lawrence, Flaubert creates Hemingway, Jane Austen's character studies lead to Henry James, the Beats would never have existed had it not been for the triumphant and gargantuan Walt Whitman, James Joyce creates Malcolm Lowry and Samuel Beckett and the entire gang of Postmodernists, *Tristram Shandy* makes possible everything, and, as my professor at NYU Harold Bloom says, Shakespeare—the greatest experimental writer ever—created us all.

The literary form we call the short story, as I have said, is a quaint relic from bygone times. This does not mean it is without use. The short story is the training ground of the novelist. It's where the novelist hones his skills.

Without experimentation Realism in all its forms stagnates. *14 Fictional Positions* is the record of one author's attempts at expanding and enhancing his lifelong mimetic fictional position.

Hope, Among Other Vices and Virtues

Charity

Four years ago, Duke, my neighbor and employer's husband, introduced me to Agnes, my employer's daughter.

Duke did this before he was my friend.

Agnes said, "I like you. You are everything in a man I want to change."

My employer and her daughter, Agnes, live down the street from the apartment complex in which Duke and I lease one-room flats. The women live in the house Duke built.

When we look out the window of Duke's flat, we see the house he built. Magnolias spread over the lawn. The branches of live oaks arc over the cobbled street of our Texas town.

"I planted the live oaks when Agnes was born," Duke says. "The magnolias when my spouse severed our relations."

When the wind blows, Duke and I watch loose shingles on the roof flutter like a stadium of applauding hands.

Envy

From the window of Duke's flat we see the women attempt to leave for shopping. We see them try to start the car and find the battery dead, their looks of frustration, their trek back inside the house, where they use the telephone to call Duke and me.

Duke and I do not answer our telephones.

Because we do not answer our telephones, the women sneak up on our apartment complex, in hopes of catching us boozing.

The women are dismayed when Duke and I booze, either independently, or, as is our custom, in manly tandem. They are dismayed when we go to the shooting range together. They are dismayed by the relative proximity of our flats.

They suspect us of covering for each other when we do things we should not be doing.

"'When armies are mobilized and issues joined,'" Duke says, "'the man who is sorry over the fact will win.' Lao-Tzu."

"Life is a hair shirt," I concur.

Lust

We live in a difficult situation, Duke and I. His spouse will not divorce him, and yet she will not grant him admission to enjoy the luxuries of her bedroom.

Agnes, Duke's daughter and the daughter of my employer, refuses, like her mother to Duke, to grant me the use of her feminine upholstery. Although we terminated our courtship four years ago, she continues as if we had not.

With great tact I have suggested that our acquaintance has outlived its pleasantness, though I have not told her, "*In ferrum pro libertate ruebant.*"

I have not told her, "My digestion gives me great concern, these days."

I fully intend to tell Agnes these things, eventually, and with effusion.

Agnes's mother, however, is my employer.

Wrath

No quantity of flowers can temper the wrath of Agnes.

The wrath of Agnes can be overt at times, subtle at others. One time, during the second year of our acquaintance, Agnes put Bessie Mae Smith on the record player.

I knew what that meant.

"I know what this means," I said.

Agnes pretended she did not understand.

When I informed Duke of the incident, he poured gin, our beverage of choice.

He played his Furtwängler *Rheingold*, and he closed his eyes, not unemotionally.

Duke handed me the gin tumbler and shook his head.

"You have my complete sympathy," Duke said. "In this matter."

Sloth

Agnes liked me when we first met. I boozed with great zeal, at that time. Then she stopped liking me.

She asked me to stop boozing.

"I will like you more," she asserted, "when you stop boozing."

I stopped boozing, mostly. Still Agnes did not like me.

I booze with Duke. Agnes suspects this, but can prove nothing.

Although she will not admit me to the diamond-tucks of her custom upholstery, she forbids me the company of other women. Nights, she walks outside my window, spying on me.

When she believes she sees me doing something I should not be doing, she drops by unannounced, if uninvited. She searches my apartment for women and booze, and when she finds my booze, hidden beneath my mattress, she pours it down the sink with great ceremony.

I am a tidy person.

I am not one to keep my women hidden beneath a mattress—

Justice

—though I do my utmost to hide them other places.

Early in the third year of my acquaintance with Agnes, I brought a woman to my flat. To show her my platyhelminth collection, and other wares equally of note.

A knocking on my door interrupted a considerable examination of gephyreoids both rare and of common variety.

"We should remain quiet," I told the woman. "Quiet is best, at such times."

I took her in my arms, with expression.

The knocking continued, and was soon enharmonied by a voice both shrill and familiar.

"He's showing you his prize nemathelminthes, no doubt," Agnes screamed.

The woman recoiled, and I was obliged to release her from my expressive embrace.

After the woman made her exit, Agnes made her entrance.

Agnes discovered my distilled spirits, beneath my mattress. She stood over my sink, pouring.

"You have flubbed an opportunity," Agnes said. "I was contraceptually prepared."

I rearranged my platyhelminth collection.

Dread rose in delicate tendrils from the sump-tank of my soul.

Prudence

I keep my booze at Duke's now, as his wife, my employer, has not been inside his flat these past fifteen years, since the day she found it for him. At Duke's, my booze rests undetected.

When I am sure Agnes is asleep, I go to Duke's. We drink until the morning train rattles down the tracks behind our flats. Then we go to work. By the time we get home from work, we are both sober enough to face the women, if we are beckoned to do so.

"Why do we live like this?"

"The examined life," Duke says, "is not worth living."

Gluttony

Agnes stops by my flat, unannounced and uninvited. She is wearing makeup, and her clothing is uncharacteristically fashionable.

"I bought new lingerie," she says. "May I come in?"

Inside, Agnes walks my flat as if a model on a runway. Agnes takes off her skirt and unbuttons her sheer blouse.

"So," Agnes says. "What do you think?"

I approach alluringly, seductively, some would say expertly. My Florsheims are polished like onyx, and their squeaks are not inaudible.

Agnes buttons her blouse and pulls up her skirt. She zips with great ceremony.

"All you want me for is sex," Agnes says.

Agnes looks at herself in the mirror.

"I understand," Agnes says, "though I do not approve."

I believe I should say something.

I consider my options and the possibilities of interpretation thereof.

I say nothing.

Temperance

Duke is a maker of bullets and a reloader of shotgun shells. Every day when Duke goes to the range to test out a new bullet or a new powder, he saves his brass and his shells and brings them home for reloading.

Duke is concerned with environmental waste.

Sometimes Duke takes me to the range. He brings his pistols and rifles and shotguns and we shoot at targets or clay pigeons. Duke can hit the clay pigeons with his pistols.

Duke is a very good shot.

"From a hundred yards," Duke says, looking at the house he built, "I could hit a diamond in a goat's ass."

Pride

"Why your acute interest in ammunition?" I ask.

"I am in search of the perfect bullet," Duke responds.

Faith

Not long ago, Duke's spouse, my employer, and her daughter, Agnes, spend the evening at St. Anthony's, the local branch of the Catholic church, where they drink wine.

"Wine is alcohol," I note. "Do you not find your stance concerning my occasional alcoholic beverage in conflict with an activity of which you are soon to partake?"

Agnes touches the cue-lever of her phonograph, on which Bessie Mae Smith already rests spinning on the platter.

My aversion to the singer grows like a well-fertilized wart on the nose of my indignity.

At the bar, Duke and I use cash. Credit card bills have been used as evidence of moral turpitude, though they prove nothing conclusively.

We do not speak of the women.

Instead, Duke breaks three snifters over the brows of impolite patrons, as a favor to the effeminate mustached barkeep.

The barkeep, without expressing gratitude, requests we quit the premises. As we begin our departure, Duke notes a cardboard placard of the entertainer Elvira, dressed in tight black satin, propped abundantly by the door.

In Duke's flat the telephone rings without let and we sit in clandestine darkness, Duke and the cardboard Elvira at his ammunition table, myself in a strategically placed folding chair by the window, looking down the street at Duke's house.

Duke duct-tapes an Astra .44 snubnose revolver to Elvira's shapely cardboard hand.

On his knees, Duke begs for assistance. Elvira does not comply, and Duke pours a gin and turns out the light.

"'If your position is formless,'" Duke says, "'the most carefully concealed spies will not be able to get a look at it, and the wisest counselors will not be able to lay plans against it.' Sun-Tzu."

"There are oil slicks in the harbor," I agree, "but that is preferable to periscopes."

Avarice

"I want a bevy of zoot-suited handmaidens to jitterbug around my flat while I play Charlie Parker tunes on a throat-warbler and drink fruity rum-based cocktails."

Fortitude

Accompanied by my employer, Agnes has decided upon a China pattern. A tastefully spare floral design, I have been informed.

I do not question their taste, in these matters.

"'There are men in the world who derive as stern an exaltation from the proximity of disaster and ruin, as others from success,'" Duke says. "Churchill."

"It's better to be shot by the wrong gun," I reply, "than not to be shot at all."

Hope

At times, when we booze, we hope the situation will change, Duke and I.

The Professor Asks His Students
If They Agree With The Conclusion:
The Table Is An Imitation
And Therefore Not Real

Now that you have heard the argument, do you agree with the conclusion, asks the professor.

I agree.

Yes; I should imagine so.

There is harmony in that, no one can deny it.

That is very true.

That is well and truly said, Socrates.

Certainly.

Yes, beyond a doubt.

Phaedo lays his head on the table, goes to sleep.

There can be no other alternative, Socrates.

Yes, Socrates; that will clearly be the answer.

Yes.

Yes.

Yes; that is what the authorities say.

What a singular dream, Socrates.

I think that you are right, Socrates; how then shall we proceed?

Crito reaches across the table, scrapes his hand, and now he has a sliver beneath his flesh.

Nothing can be clearer, Socrates.

Doubtless.

Indeed it is so.

Without further debate I can see it is so.

Granted; it is so.

Even the gods on Olympus must see it is so.

Even in Sparta they will agree it is so.

Meletus picks his nose. He rolls a substantial booger between his index finger and thumb, applies it to the underside of the table.

Not only in Sparta will they agree, Socrates, but all over lands yet unexplored they will know the verity of your conclusion.

Even those wading in the waters of Lethe will come to agree with you, Socrates.

A tanned boy, no name, enters the room. Socrates and his students all fall silent. They turn and look. The boy climbs atop the table and gets down on all fours. The professor goes first.

Well done Socrates.

We can be but imitations of this ethereal ideal.

Certainly it is so.

It cannot be refuted.

Now that you have asserted your authority over the argument, Socrates, even Xanthippe will see it is surely the best.

By far the best.

Yes; by far the best.

There can be nothing better.

In the superlative, Socrates.

I think that a good many doubts are no longer apparent, Socrates.

Yes, that was a mighty wave which you have escaped.

The students now take their turns. When they are through, the boy drops his tunic back down and leaves.

So then, you have indicated beyond a doubt that you agree that I have proved my argument, that it is the best, asks the professor.

Yes.

Yes yes.

Yes yes yes.

Yes, that must be so if the breed of the guardians is to be kept pure.

Plato has used his notes to wipe up the table. He has no more parchment on which to write, and instead carves his notes into the tabletop, to be transcribed at a later date.

HANGMAN

I

the day of the execution

The rope is snug about your perspiring neck, Aveiro Ilhavo Figueira de Foz, and we only await the final nod from the constable. I, Castelo, watch the newly laundered black sack puffing in and out like a miniature bellows as you breathe. You ask me to cut you some slack, as you prefer a quick easy snap over a lingering asphyxiation. I do not reply. Surely you must have known it would come to this if you were ever to return. But you evidently preferred to live in your world of fiction, of fantasy, of illusion. This is the price, my lover, that you must pay. Your mother and father may have told you this when punishing you as a child, but it seems especially fitting at this point in time, so I will say it, though it may seem cliché: this pains me as much as it pains you.

Together we brought this on. And when you returned, you claimed to know nothing! They asked me if I remembered the details, if I could fill in the blank spaces. I, Castelo, said I did not and could not. I tried not to disclose that which only you and I had knowledge of: our affair, your plans, your dreams. But I was weak, and I betrayed you. The spaces have been filled, the scaffold will not go unused. I know that you may never forgive me. I will, if the constable looks away, cut you some slack.

II

a time before the execution—Castelo's lament

You are asking me in this communication if I, Castelo Sabugal Guarda, believe you; and of course you know that my answer is no I do not. For how could I? It is not my duty to believe you, but rather yours to believe me.

I rest my hands on the crude windowsill and look out at the tips of celery and waves of grass, and I know that someday, like you, I too will leave this farm. You say you have seen so many wonderful things. I do want to believe you.

Yesterday afternoon was like a rebirth for me. In the neighboring village of Juarihuantas, a man stopped me. He was chewing on coca leaves and wearing an expensive sombrero. He asked if I knew a man named Carlos. And of course I thought of you, Aveiro Ilhavo, off on your journey, of your parting words as you left me. You turned to me by the well in the village, the large hat you so carefully wove using straw from the farm covering your dark eyes, and whispered so that the children and women would not hear, "Do not ever confess what we have done, for it would surely spell disaster. Will you not come with me over the mountains and into the world?" As if I had any choice? What did you think that I would do? You should be happy with me, though, for as I have imagined the wonderful places you have been since you left, the sandy beaches, the green hills, the trees as wide as huts, the snow covered mountains, I have added to the model of the world which you started building outside our hut, just below the windowsill where I can always gaze at it. I have not been to town since you left, and surely it is believed by many that I have died, or that I have gone in search of you.

Let us switch positions for the time being, so that you may feel the full import of my leaf-fringed legend.

Imagine that you, Aveiro Ilhavo, are in love with the prostitute. And she, in turn, is in love with you. Each night you stand outside her home by the river, just outside of the village, waiting for Ophiuchus to rise in the summer skies and line up parallel with the cock on the weather vane. Then it is time for you. You have already been waiting for many hours, since dusk perhaps, and you have seen many people whom you know from the farms and the village entering and later coming out. But you are not dismayed. Your special time is soon to arrive. And you know what will happen, for you have done this before. You will see the light brighten in the windows, and you will see her silhouette passing back and forth like a pacing spectre. Your heart will race, and you will be both afraid and happy at the same time. You will glance up at Ophiuchus and see that the time has come, and you will be reminded of the joke you so often tell when you are in your shanty alone. And of course, you laugh. It is the joke of a rich Brazilian who is walking on the sandy beaches of Sasso Fetore. He comes upon a pauper dressed in rags, sand clinging to his once wet clothes and skin. Look at you, just lying there, he says. I was once like you, but I made something of myself. I went to America with nothing and built myself a pushcart out of which I sold lunchfoods. After many years, I was the owner of the largest food chain in the province, Senhor Silva's. And now, I travel the world, dine in the finest restaurants, have my pick of the beautiful women, smoke the finest tobaccos. Now I can lie on this white sandy beach and relax, no cares, no problems, anytime I wish. When the rich Brazilian finishes the story of his successes, the pauper turns to him and says, "But senhor, I can already lie on this white sandy beach, and I have had to do nothing!" It is your favorite joke, and just thinking about it makes you quake in laughter. And you slip your hand into your trousers and look back at the window, then at the weathervane. It is your special time. What then do you do?

Do you:

think about the girls at the well in town, their loose garments being blown against their bodies, clinging in the wind?

tell yourself that the reason the woman you love will not make love to you is because she loves you so much?

wonder why it is that you do your most philosophical thinking while you are defecating?

think about opening your own restaurant in America?

grip tighter?

quake in laughter?

confess?

Of course, you do none of these. For it is not you who are participating in this, nor even imagining this. Do you forget? We traded places long ago, and this imagining is not yours, but mine for you to imagine. Did you believe me? How foolish of you if you did, for as I told you, I, Castelo, can never believe you, and if I cannot, how then can you be so bold as to think that I would return my disbelief with a truth?

Nevertheless I shall continue with my tale.

My hands creep along the windowsill, first one way, then the other, brittle chips of paint peeling off and falling to the dust outside. A parade of virgins and married women kick up the dust in the dead field, beads of perspiration like muddy streams on their naked bellies. They laugh at me. I put my hand in my trousers, like you did. I want to love them, and they want to love me. But they will not confess it. I grip tighter. I laugh. I think about the well in town. I think of you. I dream of the prostitute.

Women are like Americans: they all look the same.

And I do know of America, for I have read the work of Alexis de Toqueville, the book you so kindly left for me to read during your absence. I have read the book well.

The well was surrounded by women the morning that you were leaving Juarihantas, the animals sucking at the muddy earth at the base of the well, children chewing their mothers' teats, the wooden bucket rising, spilling its contents, then plunging again. You had asked me to come with you, to leave this place and seek the mysteries and treasures of the world, all the time knowing that I would not come. I hated you for asking. And the way you would draw maps in the dust, pointing out where the waters were, making mountain ranges out of little pebbles and pieces of clay, and you would look at me and smile, pointing at the stick which was you, moving it across the clay and pebbles and into lands unknown, into the finely strewn hay which you have designated as the great plains of America. Each day as the sun was setting and the mosquitoes were beginning to swirl in clouds, you would add to your relief map of the world, showing me yet another place you would someday go. And then you left.

Pause for a moment to consider what is left for Castelo.

Imagine that you once again are Castelo, and you are huddled in the bushes outside the house of the prostitute. Ophiuchus is lined up with the cock which is now spinning in the warm night breeze, the villagers and farm people are home in bed, and she is waiting for you. You loosen your grip and pull your hand out of your trousers. You can imagine what she looks like without even closing your eyes, the mussed dark hair, oily with sweat and dust, the tattered gown she has put on for comfort (her working gown now soaking in the soapy water,) the glass of water in her hand, the fingers loosely wrapped, gently shifting like waves across the glass, the cigarette in her mouth, dangling, ashes falling between her breasts like brittle leaves into a canyon. You close your eyes and she disappears.

The breeze whistles through the grass, playing a song that Castelo has come to detest.

While you are trying to imagine her again, the song wisps through the grass, the leaves, the tattered gown, the space between her breasts. You falter during your attempt to stand, to reveal yourself, afraid of what your special time holds for you tonight. You stand with your knees half bent, hunching forward, looking at the window, the weather vane, the mansard roof. You thrust your hand back into your trousers and sit back down. You detest the song that the wind plays through the blades of grass.

But you, Aveiro Ilhavo, can only imagine her, the musky odor she gives off, her low hoarse voice.

The house with the mansard is very far from where you are now.

Do you remember the night that we so desperately wished to see ourselves instead of always each other? It was dark and we had no mirror, no glass, no shiny metal surface to gaze upon. We went down to the well where mud encircles the stone barrier like the corona around the sun, gradually getting drier as the distance decreases between the well and the scattered huts of the important villagers. It was all your idea, Aveiro Ilhavo Figueira de Foz. We neglected the dark clouds which hid the stars and moon that night, and we lay down face first in the mud, our heads touching each others' and the stone barrier at the same time. It smelled of urine and dung and I lifted my face much sooner than you did. My impression in the mud was not pure, and did not look much like me, the nose and chin much flatter than my own, eyes like wide holes, no lips or mouth, only a flat space between the flat nose and flat chin. You left your face in the mud much longer than I. You lifted yourself up and regarded the perfection of the likeness. You were fortunate enough to behold yourself. Our faces were both muddied, stinking of urine and dung, but to you it was worth the while. What was once only one you of flesh was now two Aveiro Ilhavo's of mud, one standing, one lying, forming a 90` x-y axis, the feet meeting at zero. But the spectacle was fleeting, as we had forgotten the dark clouds. It began to rain. The edges of the impression eroded first, small clumps of mud and clay and sand falling into the now filling puddles. We saw islands and continents erode into the vastness of ocean. Your face began to run, mud oozing down the crevices beneath your eyes, to the sides of your mouth, and you told me that my face too was running. We stood there watching the impressions, your perfect one and my imperfect one, both become effaced. We were left only with each others' streaked faces and bodies. Our eyes were blurred and crusted, but neither of us raised a hand to wipe our eyes and improve our vision.

I lean slightly forward, my head just outside the window frame, my hands clutching the windowsill for balance. The wind is blowing harder now, the grass bent, dust obscuring the distant spires of the village, the great mountains, the eucalyptus trees by the river, the cold iron pole which proudly displays our flag, the symbol of our revolution. My eyes water. I clench them shut, then strain to open them again. The ground rumbles as if a foreign army is marching toward my hut. Squinting, I look down at the earth map. I see that the straw which was the great plains of America has blown across the rocks and pebbles and come to rest on the other side of the range of mountains. I think to replant it and restore it to its proper position, but I do not. I merely reverse my conception of that region and displace you.

(*Runs hands along windowsill. Wind blows dust into the room. Voices whisper nearly inaudibly, windlike. Light dims. Voices become increasingly louder, the sound of the wind fades.*)

The earth map.
Blurred vision.
The waves of grass.
The parade of virgins and married women.
Detested songs.
The prostitute.
Eroding faces.

You.

The cock on the weathervane.

Ophiuchus.

Me.

The windowsill.

Dust.

III

renegade in america—Aveiro Ilhavo the unclean

I sincerely hope that you will understand the things that I am to tell you. So many wonderful things I have seen since I left Juarihuantas. I do hope that I can explain this in terms which you can understand, in terms so explicit that all the spaces in your imagination will be filled. You may not believe me, but what I say is the truth. I know. It happened to me. This you can believe, Castelo Sabugal.

The cities are large. Juarihuantas houses fewer people than one building does here. The women are harlots. There are no virgins. There are no married women. Rats follow the harlots down the garbage strewn streets and into their numbered sewers. White faces. Like cocaine. Their faces have many welts and sores. I, Aveiro Ilhavo Figueira de Foz, live on the street of harlots.

I stand here in this doorway day and night. I need not move. These people bring me all I need. They lay it before me: food, drink, women women women—more than I could ever satisfy. It is a vantage point beyond compare. It is here that I see the marvelous things I tell you about. The air is warm. Hot and steaming. Even at night, when fog coats the city like a cloud of dust and insects, the heat does not wane. And if I ever become bored, I surely will think of you, Castelo. There is much, however, to consider here. There is little time.

You must come someday.

I gaze at the billboard across the street from my doorway. On it is a beautiful woman, blond, skin as dark as my own. She beckons to me with her index finger. She is not ashamed to show an abundance of cleavage. I know that I could easily love her, as she so obviously loves me. I also know that I am as close to knowing her as I am to being with you. You are not with me. You would not come. I do not know you any longer. The blond woman's index finger, though suspended for eternity in its thrusting position, is more real to me than you are.

A group of school children once gathered beneath the shelter of my doorway, uncaring of my need for an unobstructed view of the billboard woman and her beckoning finger, her wanting eyes. They started to play a game, the likes of which I had never seen in Juarihuantas. They formed a circle on the ground. The leader produced a stick of chalk. He closed his eyes and bowed his head as if in prayer (placing his four fingers on his forehead, thumb on his chin). When he came out of his meditation, he scribed seven dashes on the ground, like this:

— — — — — — —

He then drew this:

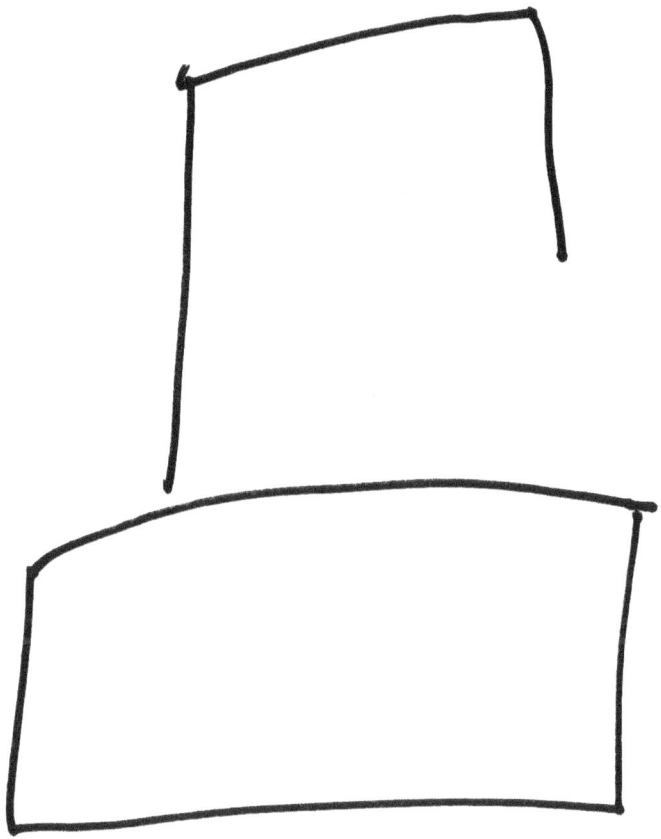

The subordinates began calling out sounds, fragments of their language, after each of which the leader would look to the sky, his index finger to his temple. Then he would shake his head and etch a body part on the sidewalk with his stick of chalk: head, body, legs, arms, fingers, toes.

The subordinates grew unruly. No matter how hard they tried, they could fill none of the spaces with their sounds. They threatened the leader, and demanded the truth, the secret of the blank spaces. But he would not succumb. He pocketed his chalk and fled.

He left the blank spaces and the drawing for me to study.

Have you been adding to our model? Have you been true to me, or have you altered it and made the model what you wish it to be? Here are my latest instructions:

 —south of the pebbles place a snail shell (this is my home)
 —burn the straw (the grain has been harvested)
 —urinate daily on the snail shell (a river flows beneath all great cities)
 —gather more twigs and lay them side by side, as closely as you can
 —lay one dead fish in the middle of the twigs.

I can not hear footsteps over the rumble of the streets; it is too dark to see shadows, the buildings looming high above, obscuring the sun. The city reeks of dead fish and mantling ponds of water. All I can perceive is that which enters the rectangle of space which I perceive through my doorway. It is certainly enough.

When I dream of Castelo Sabugal and of my faraway home in Juarihuantas, I do not wish to be distracted by the sights before me; and, as you know, I do not like to fantasize with my eyes closed. I hang a soiled towel over my face and gaze through a sea of white and black and brown, changing my focus and imagining the stains to be that which I am dreaming of: the morning fog loafing amongst the fields; the scaffold in the center of the village across from the well; hot afternoon dust sheeting over the huts in waves; wedding dresses; light brown breasts; reptiles sunning their scales on rocks; the sharp instruments of the village physician; you.

I was interrupted from a dream once, and I could not stop shaking, for the dream was of a great intensity. I do not remember the particulars, as they became instantly obscured when I snapped unwillingly into consciousness. My towel was lifted from my face, and a black man stood before me, his arm stretched across my vision, the towel in his large hand. "What 'choo be doin', man? You be missin' the show!" he said. "I beg your pardon, senhor?" I inquired. Then he pointed out the great bridge in the distance which spanned the river, explaining the virtues of its girders of steel and pillars of the strongest stone. He told me he was a stock broker, and that for a small sum I could be a shareowner of the monstrous bridge. I looked him sternly in his blood rimmed brown eyes and said no thank you, sir. I pulled the towel back over my eyes and tried to remember my fantasies, or to start a new one.

I was not born yesterday afternoon.

Have you ever seen a black man? Their eyes float in pools of blood like bloated yellow corpses. Their tongues seem pinker than ours. Their hands are softer to the touch. Many wear a peculiar costume, consisting of a blue tailed coat, yellow waist-coat, and trousers with high black boots. There are many of them here, in front of my doorway, passing by again and again. The youths of the race are plagued by an odd form of epilepsy, and it is not uncommon to see a crowd gather around a stricken child who is shuddering and having spasms as if possessed by evil demons, or the ague. And the crowd smiles and seemingly takes the fit for a festive occasion.

What if the Catholics are right about everything, I mean *everything*? If all that the very reverend Father Sorrel says is absolutely true? It would be a certainty that you and I would suffer for what we have done. Should we not then partake of the joys which are offered us to their fullest? Is there any reason that we are suffering this pitiful separation?

Join me.

The final leg of my journey here was in an automobile with a host of young Americans. They called the car a Hudson and said that they had found "IT" at a whorehouse, and to them this was very amusing. Has the prostitute let you lay your flesh upon hers, or are you still devising your plan? Do you crouch nightly behind the bushes in wait? Castelo, my lover, the stars are different and fewer here. Ophiuchus is not in the skies. If you were to wait here for your special time, it would either never come or it would be constantly upon you. You would then be forced to act. Would you? I do not believe that you would. I believe that you are trying to fail.

You are always asking me to imagine that I am you, and you know that I cannot, for I am not you and will never be. I do not want to be you. I do not want to fail. For once, imagine that you are Aviero Ilhavo, and you have left your windowsill, the waves of grass, the house with the mansard. You have faced many perils, the crazy Americans in the Hudson, the Border Patrol, the bad water of Mexico, the tall Americans with cowboy hats and pointed boots. You are walking through the streets of a large city, pigeons gabbling along beside you, too fat to fly, lecherous women leering with lonely wanton lamentations. You are in search of a place to rest, to sit or stand without being told, "Move along spic, ain't ya got anything better to do than stand?" And of course, whenever they ask, you do not have anything better to do than stand, so you must move along. The motion to you means nothing. You read the signs as you walk, though you do not understand all of the words:

H   elp Wanted

A   rmy Navy Air Force Marines

N   o Shoes No Shirt No Service

G   od Saves

M   en At Work

A   nimal Shelter

N   o Loitering

You stop a woman and ask her to help you read the signs. "Can you help me read the signs?" you ask. "It depends on which ones," she says and continues walking down the street. She has many welts and sores on her face, and her voice is offensive, sour like grapefruit just picked, and she emits an odor which can only be the combined fume of all of the men in her life, lingering long after she has moved deftly on. She does, however, have large breasts which do not sag much.

At times I feel like a man lying on my back in the dark.

She reminds you of when you were a child. Your babysitter too had large breasts. She showed them to you once. You did not want to see them. She tied you up like a sow with rope, and you did not close your eyes, though you think you wanted to. Your feet and hands were tingling and numb, a result of the tightness of the rope which bound together your wrists and ankles. Do you like to look at these? she asked. Do you do you do you? You did not answer, but you did look at them, the way they bobbed up and down in her cupped hands, the way the skin bulged out between her widespread fingers, the three long black hairs on the left nipple waving like tiny flagellites in the opposite motion of the alternately bobbing dugs.

(Thrusts hand into trousers. A horn blows in the distance. The graffiti papered walls surrounding on all sides flutter in a sudden gust of wind. Dashes head against several different photo advertisements depicting women in submissive positions. Moves hand increasingly faster in many differing positions. A host of onlookers appear on the street and sidewalk, watching in mute ennui. The sound of the horn gradually fades. Pulls soiled towel from back pocket with free hand and places it atop head. Eyes disappear from view of the crowd. The people in the crowd all turn and stare at the billboard with the beckoning blond woman, and, in unison, raise their arms and point their index fingers at her.)

IV

the day of the execution—Castelo's apology

We should never have traded places. I told you it would not be a good thing. Now look: everything is confused. And if I had it all to do over again, I surely would do it differently. Do you remember the day when we were exposed? The day when I, Castelo, confessed despite your pleas and supplications? It might have been a Wednesday, though any day of the week that I tell you, you will believe.

The villagers of Juarihuantas and the other neighboring villages were gathered around the well. There were so many people, along with their animals and children, that even the seldom used scaffold was creaking under the weight, as there was no more room to stand on the ground. And in the middle you stood, Aviero Ilhavo Figueira de Foz, like a god returned from the heavens or like a proud warrior returned from battle. Your clothes were strange, and to show your newfound wisdom, you spoke the strange language you had learned. How could we simple villagers not be frozen in awe?

Imagine that you were in the place of Castelo, and it was you who had been witness to what Aveiro Ilhavo had done. You would have been hunched outside the window of the prostitute, hidden in the low thicket, your hand buried in your trousers, waiting for Ophiuchus. It was a cloudy night, and the constellations were hidden, but you would have known when your time had arrived: four minutes later than the night before. This night, you were certain, was to be the night when you at last actualized your desires, when you summoned the courage to answer to the beckon of the prostitute, to her long white finger which you fancied first pointed toward you, then curled in toward the chasm between her sun white breasts.

How would you have prepared yourself for what you then would have seen? When you saw me in her sacred chamber, actualizing your long latent love, my chest wet with sticky beads of moisture, my blood welling up; and her, the prostitute, in her thinnest finery, sunk deep into her down chair in wait, preparing herself—what would you have done?

Would you have:

run back to the hut and made wreckage of the earth map?

slowly retracted your hand from your trousers and examined it in the dim light of the moon-refracting cloud mist?

destroyed *La Democracie en Amerique* by incineration, laceration, or page by page shredding?

repeated your favorite jingle and attempted to quake in laughter, only to find your attempt failing feebly?

confessed?

revealed to the villagers of Juarihuantas the secret, embodying all possible hyperbole of the facts, crying for the long unused scaffold to be set once again into use?

watched as I destroyed you?

The choice is for you to make.

I, Castelo, am the hangman, employed to execute condemned prisoners by hanging.

This is not merely a children's game in which blank spaces are filled with letters to create a word. For each wrong choice, one body part is added to the stickman on the scaffold; for each correct choice, one letter is revealed.

And now how does the rope about your neck feel? Is it perhaps a bit too snug? For once you say nothing. Are you remembering our separation? You can not see through the black cloth sack, but if you could, you would see the prostitute. She is watching you and me, together on the scaffold. She does not weep. Her skin looks much different in the sunlight. It resembles the harlotskin you once described to me, when I had no desire to hear of it. But you were relentless. You filled me with unneeded descriptions, and now you feel the weight of what words can do.

Third Person On A Bed Built For Five

A declawed cat walks across the living room floor, ashtray strapped to its back. It does not mind the ashtray. It has been to parties before.

When I was seven years until I was ten years old, I would play chess with my father. I always beat him. We switched to checkers. But I always beat him at that too.

The cat walks back across the room. It scratches its paws on the scratchpost, shag rug on a fat dowel. It walks back across the room in futility.

A frequented mode of expression, he said. Stock.

Do you want white or black?

I am in the dorian mode for the time being, natural minor.

No, he decided not to come, wanted to play with his computer, he and it, together.

What are you writing, Jeremy?

A drunken handwriting analysis to be soon typeset, proofread, published, distributed, and plastered on dormitory walls all over the nation.

Life is great material, said the writer.

Here kitty kitty. Here, kitty.

The great floppy disc upstairs, double sided, double density, formatted, but all his files are empty.

And I felt my glasses, and they were bent, and I didn't know how they got bent, and I knew that I must have missed something.

He sits there in front of that screen all day. If he's not trying to write, he's playing a video game to pass the time.

The declawed cat walks back across the room. —The ashtray is full now.

When I was ten, just before my eleventh birthday, he beat me at checkers. He hasn't played me since.

And I always find him sitting there, punching the escape key, again, and again, and again.

Do you know how the game of chess began?

And it just brings him back to the main menu, the list.

Check.

He refused to reply abruptly.

Do you have a towel, he ejaculated.

Jeremy sits there with a pen, the thief.

The audience was hesitant, even reluctant, to speak. Jeremy took notes on the silence.

The literature of silence, Samuel Beckett, the scriptures, said the writer.

If you are a writer life is a tax deduction.

He put the cigarette in the center of the table in the ashtray in the slot, carefully. He put it in backwards.

I always ask him to play, but he still won't.

They used to use real people, moved by dignitaries with megaphones. Kings, popes, et cetera.

When the cigarette burned down, the ashes fell on the fur of the declawed cat. The cat did not notice.

Check.

It's a new video game, nuclear warfare it's called. If you lose, you go to the fallout shelter, furnished, stocked, heated, cooled, carpeted, plumbing functional, in the cellar of the library of congress.

Here kitty kitty. Here kitty.

They used to battle for the squares with swords.

Check.

But if you lose, you end up on the surface of the planet, standing in a wheat field, melting down with the cows, the geese, the horses, the termites, the pigs.

The winner got to stand on the square, now claimed for the dignitary.

He just smiles and laughs when I ask him. Someday, he says.

Either way you lose your quarter.

Mate.

I am the third person. I am the third person on a bed built for five. I go to parties often. Two couples and me usually. Where is Jeremy, they asked. Masturbating in the bathroom, taking notes with his spare hand. I bet he's got a mouthful on us.

Has anybody seen the ashtray, she asked. Here kitty.

It's much too quiet here.

Like, it's hard, she said, you know, like, you know, it's hard, you know, to make a decision, like, you know? Are you an athlete, she asked.

Does it occur to you that I may be otherwise, in a different mode, the locrian perhaps, the half diminished chord or scale beginning on the seventh degree, on a skew plane, outside, I asked.

Being stood up on a date. Going to a party uninvited.

She laughed.

A skew set of lines in an indeterminate plane.

Creusa

Many times after he had cleaned his brushes and scrubbed the oils and acrylics from his face Romero had walked below her second-floor hotel room on Toulouse Street on his way to his favorite bar, The Dungeon. He had heard the sound of a flute playing solo and had thought the player very skilled. Sometimes Romero would stop and stand and he would listen in the humid delta night for a long time, wiping hot pools of perspiration from his forehead with his forearm. He would listen to the flute whistle low beneath the electric whirring of the cicadas and he would wonder if he could paint the song the flute was playing, if he could make the oils swirl and trill and crescendo and diminuendo and dance like notes of color yet still represent something from nature. If he could paint like the flute played he would paint something very good.

But Romero could not tell what it was about the flute's songs he liked so much, why they were so different from his own work; he didn't even know what songs they were, who wrote them, where they came from. Perhaps it was that though the flute was a tangible thing, the music was not. Perhaps that was why he liked the songs. Romero used paint and brushes and canvas and when he was through the finished product was just a rearrangement of things that already existed. But the music, once played, was gone, and existed only in the infinitely resonating echoes of memory and space. Romero did not like to think about this too much because he had not yet even perfected his own imperfect medium, so most of the time he did not stand and listen for a long time.

Romero had never actually seen her, but the nights he walked home from the bar instead of driving he would see her vaguely defined silhouette passing back and forth across the sun-browned window shades and she would still be playing. All the while he had been drinking Scotch in The Dungeon she had been creating, and none of it was left. Why isn't she playing somewhere where people can enjoy her music, Romero wondered. He had always thought of art as something that needed an audience, that wasn't complete until it had stood the test of criticism, and that was why he thought it so important that he someday paint a very good painting again and let people see that he still had it in him to paint a very good painting. He had always thought that art wasn't art until someone else had perceived it, that art could not exist in a vacuum, that creating art for only one's self was the lowest form of masturbation. But the girl with the flute was not playing for anyone, so far as Romero could tell, and yet he could not think of her music as anything but art. And if what she was doing was art, then what was his work? Many times Romero had stopped in front of her house after drinking many Scotches and listened to her music and he had studied her vaguely defined silhouette.

Romero could not tell from the silhouette how she looked, but strangely it did not seem to matter how she looked.

One night Romero decided to walk home because he needed to think and he did not want to go back to the house just yet and he was still very drunk. The streets were not quiet and he could not tell the buzz of cicadas and mosquitoes from the buzz of electric wires and neon lights.

Cars passed by and the drivers did not know who he was only that he was a man who was drunk and a man who was walking. Romero tried not to listen to the sounds of tires thumping into pot holes and prostitutes calling out of windows to other men on the streets and people laughing and sometimes not laughing. Romero was a painter and he was used to seeing and not listening, but tonight he tried not to listen and the more he tried the more he listened and all he wanted was to not hear.

Romero did not hear the flute when he reached her hotel. Her light was on but there was no silhouette and no music and still he could hear only street sounds and he did not want to hear them. He stood outside and tried not to be drunk but he was drunk anyway and still she would not play the flute. He might have said something but he could not tell if he had or not. Romero sat on the sidewalk, his back against a cold iron lightpost, and he waited for her to play.

She did not play and Romero did not know what to do because he wanted to hear her play so he walked into the lobby and up the rotting and splintering wooden stairs and he did not like the way the stairs creaked as if they would not hold his weight. He walked down the corridor and stopped at the door he thought was hers and he knocked twice.

"You may come in," came a female voice.

Romero opened the door and saw her for the first time. She sat on the bed with the flute in her lap and her feet did not touch the plywood floor. The bed was not made. She wore a long black dress and her ankles did not show. Her hair was long and stringy and bleached blond with black roots and her eyebrows were shiny black. Her eyes were painted with a great deal of makeup, not like a whore, but like an actress who had not yet cleaned up after a performance on the stage.

"You're not playing tonight," Romero said.

"I am Greek," she said.

"You play very wonderfully."

"Tonight I do not play."

"I would like it very much if you did."

"You have heard me before. You do not need to hear the flute tonight."

"Tonight I especially need to hear the flute."

"I cannot play for you to listen."

"I am Juan Romero. I am a painter."

"Yes," she said. "I am Creusa and tonight I do not play the flute."

Romero sat down in a chair and asked her if she had anything to drink and she said yes she did, she had rum. It was not good rum but it was rum and they poured drinks and they drank.

Romero wanted to paint her. He wanted to paint her with her flute and paint the music too. He drank more rum and wondered how he would do it and he thought of the painting of the whale-spouts in The Dungeon and how he did not like it now.

Creusa had not looked beautiful at first, she was short-legged and short-bodied and unathletic and her skin was the same bleached color as her hair and her skin and her hair were whiter than the exposed sheets of her bed. But now Romero studied her figure as if he were going to paint it and he saw that she had the figure of a Reubens woman or a Dürer woman and even her plumpness was very beautiful. To paint her, Romero thought, I would have to paint like she plays the flute. When I paint a subject the subject ceases to exist and only the painting remains and the painting is not the subject anymore but only paint and canvas. But to paint Creusa correctly I would have to take something from her and put it into the canvas and paint and perhaps I can not do that. She can play the flute and the music is both her self and music at the same time; but a painting—can it be both paint and her at the same time also? Juan Romero poured Creusa another rum and he poured himself another rum.

"Play your flute for me."

"I can only play if you do not listen. Promise not to listen and I will play."

"I promise."

"Then I will play," she said. "But I am not playing for you and if you listen you will not hear what I play."

"I won't listen."

She lifted the silver flute to her lips and closed her eyes and her eyeshadow glittered in the lamplight and she tilted her head down and Juan Romero watched. She held the flute in her fingers more delicately than he had ever held a brush and she blew air over the flute and the flute made no note but Romero heard the air hissing low and sure and it sounded as beautiful as a note.

She pulled the flute away and opened her eyes and she looked at Romero. "You're listening," she said.

"No I'm not," he said.

"Stop listening to my music."

"Yes," Romero said.

She played again and Juan Romero tried not to listen. Again she blew a long breath of air over the mouthpiece, but this time Romero listened to other things. He heard footsteps in the corridor outside the door and he heard a bottle break below on the street. He heard her take in air and he imagined he could hear her lungs filling beneath her dress. Someone coughed in the room next door and a door slammed shut. Romero picked at his index finger with his thumbnail and he heard the click of flesh peeling.

She was playing a long note now and he tried not to listen but it wasn't working. No matter how hard he tried to listen to certain sounds the note she was playing seemed to be the base of them all, the tone underlying all the noises of the hotel, of the city, of everything Romero could hear. She began playing different long notes, holding them longer than Romero imagined possible, especially for such a small woman. It seemed that her notes were the key in which all sounds were played and each time she changed notes the key of all sounds changed at her command.

She played faster and faster. Romero kept trying not to listen and he drank more rum and he did not feel very drunk anymore. He heard her fingertips sliding across the keys and he heard the keys slapping against the pads of her flute. He heard her take in air and he heard the hiss of her breath across the mouthpiece. The vibration of his ears seemed to make their own sound and the sound he heard was not only Creusa's music nor Creusa's breath but every sound humming through the New Orleans night. Romero knew that even if he wanted to he could not listen to her music alone now. Her music was no longer isolated, it was a part of something much larger. Romero could not listen much longer.

He did not realize that she had stopped when she stopped. He sat slumped in the chair and she stood over him and nudged him.

"I am finished," she said.

"I did not listen."

"Yes," she said.

"It was very nice."

"You are tired now."

"I need to rest," he said.

"We will not make love," she said. "You have heard enough for tonight."

"No," Romero said.

Phrases and Philosophies for the Use of the Young

Life is a self-paced suicide.

Historians will speak of us in the past tense.

We were once young and fresh, but now we are old and we smell.

It's better to shoot the wrong man than not to shoot at all.

Change is absolutely necessary for growth and for buying cigarets.

Sex without guilt: what's the use?

I only know what time it is when I don't have to tell somebody else.

Good digestion is the blessing of the philosopher of the stomach.

Near the end of our lives time becomes a gas and we watch and feel it dissolve.

On the interstate highway of letters, I am roadkill; in the Mexican party of life, I'm the piñata;

Failure is not as easy as it seems.

Consider the sincerity of incompetence.

Our lives are perfect spheres, and we roll from room to room.

Some of our colleagues have been incarcerated, others have not. The point is moot: we all do time.

The severest vice is a clear conscience: to overcome a vice is to murder a virtue.

Education does not help the mind much, but neither does anything else.

The only thing that gets us through the waking hours is the sleeping hours.

Sometimes a hangnail can make all the difference.

How can one enjoy oneself without offending one's self?

Psycho-sexual responses necessarily lead to cannibalism, but just try to tell that to young people.

The Winnebago of our culture is parked in a tow-away zone.

The are oil slicks in the harbor, but that is preferable to periscopes.

Armageddon: If you don't survive, so what. If you do, think of the smooth commute.

We can't help thinking we have forgotten something: the tragedy is we have not.

You can't steer a train.

To create a system is to destroy a system: destruction is the employment of the artist.

The Cow Island Open

1

Theobald Carnwad thinks about the shanty on stilts, rising out of the gray swamp. He sees the sixteenth tee of the Cow Island Open, and his shiny white Titlist sailing over the barbed-wire fence toward the wood-slat shanty.

He sees himself standing on the planked porch, looking between the gaps in the boards at the slime and water below, his clothes soaked with rich dark mud, his hand about to push open the door and reveal what is inside.

2

This is the first round of golf Theobald Carnwad has shot since the '53 Cow Island Open. That was when he sliced his shiny white Titlist off into the swamp and blew his lead over Clinton Hannah. For twenty years, Carnwad has been trying to gather the courage to play another round of golf, and today Carnwad has done it—he has spent the day on the course.

It has been a lonely day, very few other golfers, as it has recently stormed and the course is still sloppy. The sun is setting, and Carnwad has made par on the fifteenth hole.

3

Theobald Carnwad's best friend in college was Clinton Hannah, even though Carnwad hated him. Carnwad hated Hannah because Hannah beat him at everything.

Their freshman year at LSU they were roommates. They drank a great deal at the negro bars which surrounded the campus, and Hannah usually had to guide Carnwad home, because Carnwad could not drink as well as Hannah.

One time Carnwad wanted to get some exercise, so he asked Hannah to come shoot a few buckets at the basketball courts.

Carnwad was obliged to wait for Hannah, because Hannah was putting on his red silk shorts, his expensive basketball sneakers, his head and wrist bands, his numbered jersey. "I was going to play college ball," Hannah said, "but I decided on engineering instead. I got six offers from universities, you know. Marquette, UCLA, Syracuse. Decided to major in physics."

Carnwad remembered the time his mother sat him down to have a man to man talk. He remembered the look of disgust she gave him when he told her he wanted to be an accountant. "Your Daddy was a golfing man," she said. "The finest. And Big Daddy before him. They wanted you to be a golfing man too, Theobald. And just look at yourself."

Carnwad looked at himself. He looked at his belly, his oversized feet, his fat squishy fingers.

"You are the last of the Carnwad men, Theobald. Do not disappoint me, boy. Do not let down your Daddy, and Big Daddy before him. God rest their gentlemanly souls."

The day after the basketball game, Carnwad lay on his bunk watching Hannah get dressed for class. He wondered how many days would pass before he would be capable of doing the same.

"Aren't you going to class, Theo old boy?"

"Must have pulled a muscle in my back," Carnwad said. He thought about all the stairs on campus, and how he would have to clutch the bannisters just to keep from falling down.

"Darn rotten luck old boy. Darn rotten luck."

Carnwad decided to try his luck at something less physical. One day, while it was storming outside with hot delta rain, he asked Hannah if he wanted to play chess.

Hannah did not look up from his book. "I don't really like chess," he said. "It makes me tense."

Carnwad grew excited. He started talking fast. "Come on Hannah what's the matter Hannah don't want to play chess Hannah it's just a game Hannah a brain game Hannah come on!"

Carnwad was not expecting a six move checkmate. He looked at the board and tried to figure out where he had gone wrong.

"You see, Theo old boy, if you would have moved here, then I couldn't have done this."

Hannah started rearranging the board, playing a new game against himself. "And then you moved the rook here, which is always a mistake, given my opening. I was wondering what you were up to—you had me concerned. I didn't think anyone would do something like that unless they had something up their sleeve. Won a tournament in New Orleans when I was in junior high school, you know. Quit playing the circuit because it made me too tense."

When Carnwad found out that Hannah had never played golf before, he offered to teach him the game. Hannah bought clubs at a garage sale: putter, 7-iron, driver.

"Don't worry," Carnwad said, as Hannah sat steel-wooling rust from the clubs' faces. "Those are all the clubs you'll need at first."

Carnwad beat Hannah by twenty strokes their first time out. Hannah liked the game, though, and wanted to start playing every Friday after classes, which was just fine with Carnwad. Hannah was hooked. Carnwad was happy.

And Carnwad's Mama was happy, too. Carnwad was getting better and better, and half-way through winter semester his junior year, he quit and joined the PGA tour, following in the footsteps of Daddy and Big Daddy before him.

Hannah quit school, too, during his senior year, but he didn't win a tournament until the '53 Cow Island Open, when he and Carnwad were both fifty-eight years old.

4

Carnwad had always hated the sixteenth tee. It seemed like every time he drove at that hole, he sliced the ball over the low barbed-wire fence and into the swamp beyond. He would stand there, stupid, watching the little white ball curve between the cypresses and plop into the swamp. There was a rotting shanty on stilts out there, partially obscured by the moss hanging from the thin boughs of trees. Carnwad's balls seemed drawn to it like insects to a decaying carcass. There was no telling how many balls he'd lost on sixteen.

5

"We're here on the sixteenth tee of the Cow Island Open. The surprise sensation of this year's Southern States Tournament has been Theobald Carnwad, making a comeback after over twenty years off the circuit, leading his arch-rival Clinton Hannah by only one stroke. The crowd falls silent as he eyes the fairway."

"Four-wood, caddy. My Titlist, please."

"Just look at that poise, that youthful bounce. Baton Rouge must be very proud of Theobald Carnwad, its prodigal son, at seventy-eight the oldest person on the PGA tour!

"Carnwad raises his club, swings, good contact with the ball. It's heading straight, rising, curving, slicing to the right, slicing off the fairway, over the barbed-wire fence and into the swamp. Looks like it's going to plop into the water by an old shack. That ball's gone for good, and Carnwad's going to have to take a two stroke penalty. Darn rotten luck for Theobald Carnwad...."

6

His back arched like a sapling in a Louisiana hurricane, twisting, quivering and about to snap. With his 4-wood circling slowly above his head, he tried to guide the distant white Titlist back onto the fairway. Carnwad had chosen to play alone so no one would see shots like this one.

Carnwad didn't want to trudge through the swamp to retrieve his Titlist, but the sixteenth tee was a long way from the Pro Shop and it had been his last ball. He looked out at the swamp, at the sagging trees, gray Spanish moss hanging from thin boughs, the sky and mud the same dull color, no horizon, just miles and miles of endless muck and mire and moss and dead and dying trees.

Except the shanty.

The shanty shimmered like a mirage, rising out of the mud on its stilts, the reflection streaming through the trees halfway to the barbed-wire fence. Carnwad squinted, trying to see if there was anything moving inside.

7

It is the '53 Cow Island Open, and Clinton Hannah is talking to Theobald Carnwad as they walk the path to the sixteenth tee.

"Lost a lot of balls here, Theo old boy. Ever wondered why?" Hannah grinned. "Come on, Theo old boy, haven't you ever wondered why?"

Carnwad looked across the swamp at the shanty.

He looked at Hannah.

Hannah was still grinning.

8

On the first tee, Carnwad sank a thirty foot putt by hitting the Titlist extra hard to compensate for the sogged green. He used his 3-iron out of the sand trap on the fourth because he knew the wet sand wouldn't suck the ball down. But how is he supposed to finish his round without a ball?

Distraught, he watches the ball dropping, and listens for the noise it will make when it splashes down.

He straightens his back and lowers his 4-wood. His bag of clubs slung over his shoulder, Carnwad starts the long walk back to the clubhouse.

9

Carnwad remembered the '53 Cow Island Open. He was leading Clinton Hannah by only one stroke. But that was before the sixteenth tee.

Hannah's drive was strong and true, two hundred forty yards, mid-fairway.

"Four-wood, caddy. My Titlist, please," Carnwad said.

Carnwad felt the cold steel shaft in his palm. He held the club out horizontally to make sure the shaft had not incurred a warp, and when he had assured himself of its trueness, his eyes focused on the stilt-supported shanty which rose out of the swamp.

Were his eyes playing tricks on him, or was there someone watching him from inside, from between the gaps in the rotting gray wood?

When Carnwad swung, out of the corner of his eye he caught a slight movement. His shot sliced, and the ball curved over the barbed-wire fence toward the depths of the swamp.

"Darn rotten luck, old boy," Hannah said. "Darn rotten luck."

Carnwad padded to the edge of the fairway, the already moist sod becoming increasingly sloppy toward the rough. He stopped where the slick mud began. His Titlist was out there, somewhere by that shack on stilts. He stood there on the edge of the rough, his feet sinking into the warm mud until he could feel it beginning to wrap his ankles. He watched that shanty, watched the crevices and cracks in the wood.

He thought he saw something move inside, but he couldn't be sure.

10

With his hands placed between the burrs of the barbed-wire, Carnwad tries to see between the wood slats of the house on stilts.

The sun has set, and the flat gray color of the sky is darkening. The trees look like shades of the dead. Carnwad places his left foot down on the lowest wire of the fence, and with his gloved left hand lifts the next wire up. He hunches over, making himself as small as he can. Carefully, he moves his head, then his right leg, between the barbed-wires. Once on the other side, he stands, inhales the humid air deep into his lungs, and begins walking into the swamp,

toward the shanty. The mud is warm and creamy, and it feels good
on Carnwad's ankles, shins, and knees as it gets deeper and deeper.
His trousers are heavy and tighten around his thighs. Carnwad keeps
pushing through. The mud is up to Carnwad's chest, and it takes all
his strength just to keep moving. He stops to rest, mud beneath his
armpits, arms draped out in front of his body, seemingly floating on
the surface. He squishes gray noodles of mud through his fingers by
squeezing his hands into fists. It is very dark now, and Carnwad can
barely make out the silhouette of the shanty through the trees.

11

Carnwad sees a golf ball. It is only a few feet in front of his outstretched
arms, a nearly submerged white egg nestled in the gray mud. Carnwad
lunges toward the ball. The mud rolls in a slow wave. His feet are no
longer on solid bottom, and the ball moves farther away. He lunges again,
and the ball moves. Carnwad sinks deeper into the mud. He feels the mud
on his neck, beneath his chin.

He lunges.

He lunges.

He lunges…

12

Carnwad treads water below the shanty. He sees a rope-ladder
hanging from the porch and into the water. He is covered with light
gray moss, and because of the swim, the mud that once caked his
clothes and body is now a thin film of slime. His soaked undershorts
are uncomfortable, shirt clinging to his belly and shrinking around
his armpits.

After climbing the rope-ladder, he pulls himself onto the porch. The boards, old and weak, bend under his weight.

Carnwad hears something plunk into the water.

He turns around and looks back toward the course, toward the sixteenth hole.

The half-moon is just above the flag, and the flag shimmers like a distant torch fluttering in the breeze.

13

The shanty sways, making creaking and moaning noises. A gust of wind whips across the porch, across the swamp, the Spanish moss swinging from the trees. Carnwad shivers and feels goosebumps rise on his skin.

He turns and faces the door. He hesitates, then places his hand on the coarse wood. He smells the mold, the staleness, the decay. He feels the air press against his temples, wrapping his head, weighing down his shoulders, his extended arm.

Carnwad takes a long breath, and pushes open the door.

14

Carnwad sees golf balls.

No furniture, no windows, just hundreds and hundreds of old yellow golf balls covering the floor.

The door behind him swings gently back and forth in the breezes that move through the shanty. He stands, motionless, listening to the wind and the creaking of bending wood.

He walks through the golf balls to the opposite side of the room. He fits his hands into a crevice between two boards, gripping tightly with his fingers. With a jerk, he rips a board from the wall. He stands there, the broken board in his hands, looking at the dark swamp through the hole in the wall, the moon reflecting off the rippling water. He examines the board, holding it in his hands. The board is thin enough that, gripping, he can touch his fingers to his palms.

He drops the board to the floor. He starts ripping down boards, examining them, then throwing them down.

15

Carnwad has made par on the fifteenth hole. He hates the sixteenth, and, as he approaches the tee, he thinks about the '53 Cow Island Open, when he blew his lead over Clinton Hannah.

He holds the wooden tee between his index and middle fingers, thumb on top of the shiny white Titlist, and pushes the tee into the sod with the ball on top. The early evening skies are dark, and it is starting to sprinkle.

He looks at the distant flag fluttering in the wind.

He raises his 4-wood and swings.

16

Carnwad has torn a large hole in the wall of the shanty.

The hole is as wide as three doorways, and reaches from the low ceiling to the floor. He holds a board in his hands as he stands on the edge, looking down at the swamp. He has lined up the golf balls in neat rows. With the board, he leads a ball along the floor to the edge. He looks out at the swamp, focuses on a cypress stump poking out of the water like a witch's thumb. He sets his feet, positions the end of the board behind the ball, coils back, and swings, sending the ball sailing into the air, into the swamp, straight and true toward the stump.

He moves another ball to the edge, sets, and swings, watches the darkness and listens for the plop. When he hears it, he moves another ball into place. Carnwad sets and he swings.

He sets, and he swings.

Set.

Swing.

A Wise Man is Known by his Laughter

With every line I write I kill off the "artist" in me.

It's always dangerous for a writer to read too much, for a writer to spend his days and nights and dreams hashing over the works of other generations, waking up from a sleep with someone else's sentence on your lips as if speaking in tongues.

For a long time I used to keep my Proust in the bathroom next to the john, and one day, near the end of the book, I read a sentence—what sentence I don't even remember—but when I read the sentence it gave my soul a hardon. I didn't think about what a great sentence it was, how well it was constructed, what the giggling chimps in the semiotic circle-jerk would deduce about the ornate sign system; I didn't pull my leatherbound notebook from underneath the sink and copy like the sober Bartleby. No. I read the sentence over and over, and it was like an indictment, a howl from the sump-tank of my soul, a dying moan from a part of me I'd forgotten had ever been there. And I wondered what had happened to me, why my passions had withered like so many sun-shrivelled apples, why when I looked in the mirror I saw layers of perspective and vanishing points and Manet and Magritte and Velasquez and Parmigianino instead of a man of flesh and bone. My years of study rose before me like a militia of unleashed malevolent phantasms, spectres of the dictionaries, of syllabi, of humid stormy evenings that never saw the soles of my shoes.

I used to walk late in the machinery of night, and I'd walk not to examine the *langue* of the onyx-eyed natives, not to jolt myself out of an academic stupor, not as if I were on an anthropological expedition to prove a hypothesis that the world was out of whack—I'd walk because I *needed* to. I needed to move, I needed to feel my muscles heat up and stretch and feel the sights of the long dark streets that never revealed more than at night. I felt alive like I've never felt alive since, my neurons firing like hundreds of tiny gatling guns in my sinews, bulletspray of the brain. I didn't have to try to hear the rustling of paper bags blowing down the street, or the urgent spring-squeak of the lovers' rocking car. I'd walk with a sense of imminent peril, not for fear of being attacked by muggers or policemen or the Oakland stray hounds—I wasn't charged with the electricity of a virgin on a ghetto street alone, I didn't expect a car to squeal around a corner and run me down. No, I was afraid because I was alive and I knew I was alive, and because I was alive I could die any instant, not necessarily at the hand of someone else, but by the will of the gods. And I knew there were gods then: it never occurred to me that through semantic calisthenics I would someday be able to eliminate them, that I would be able to reason them out of history and out of existence. And while I was sitting there on the john, Proust on my lap, I began to weep, and I don't remember what happened next, but I ended up outside my flat in the Oakland night, standing on the creaking wooden landing, smoking cigarettes, pack after pack, and, for the first time I could remember, I watched the sun come up like a blood orange and spill its indifferent flames over the bay. And I knew that I would not sleep for days, that I'd watch the sun rise and set and rise again until my body crumpled to the earth like a heap of dirty laundry—but my mind would keep going, racing through my slumber with hooves of basalt and granite that would never let me sleep the sleep of a dead man again. A man who is alive remembers the time he is asleep as well as the time he is awake. An artist never sleeps.

Nights I lay awake wishing I were somewhere else. No matter where I am, no matter how little dissonance my domestic situation might seem to be producing—I could be camping in the Alaskan forests, low gauzey clouds and pale blue sky, the salmon browning over birch embers, or spending a night with a starry-eyed woman in the St. Francis on Knob Hill, blowing snow, standing naked in front of the 32nd floor window, exposed to the bay and the lights and the cabbies and God—it doesn't matter where I am, I always wish I were somewhere else. In this I am American. I've watched too many movies, I've listened to too many sixties weekends on the FM radio, I've read Kerouac and *Huckleberry Finn* and Melville and Henry James and Whitman. No different than any other educated American, I've vicariously lived the life of the expatriate and subvert, I've taken Odysseus as my role model, but I'm too much the coward to spend ten years adrift on the wine-dark sea, and I know that the gods of today are luetic and have crabs.

Instead of seas, I've fallen in love with asphalt and rubber; I've learned to relish the time I spend behind the wheel, at night, the windows down and the road desolate, just the air and the land and my car and me, driving.

When I was a boy and my father used to come up from Oakland and take me from my mother's in Sacramento once a month, instead of taking me to the zoo, or to a park, or to an overnight travelling carnival or to a weekend of Walt Disney movies, he used to ask me where I wanted to go. Before we'd even left my mother's apartment, he'd pull out the worn, grease-marked California map from the glove compartment of his '59 Ford and unravel it across the long bench seat. "Where?" he'd ask, and I'd close my eyes and concentrate, then raise my hand and then stab down on the paper with my index finger. And wherever my finger would land, San Diego, Alturas, Eureka, the great Sequoia forest, the wastelands of the southern central valley and its psuedo-civilized settlements of Bakersfield, Buttonwillow, Fresno, Weed Patch and Arvin, the northern California coast, or Scotty's Castle, the Tehachapi Desert, the glacial pie-slice of the Yosemite Valley, the bikini beaches of the smog-stink southern coast— wherever my finger landed that's where we'd go for the weekend. Unless, of course, my finger landed too close to Sacramento, in which case I'd have to try again. Usually, though, after at most one try, my finger would land far enough away from Sacramento that Pop and I'd spend the entire weekend driving—we'd drive a full day in one direction, turn around, and take another route back to my mother's place. We never got back before bedtime on Sunday.

Since then, I haven't been able to stand being in one place long enough to hook up the phone. When I was a teenager I'd get into my stationwagon and drive, just aim the car in a direction and go. I'd never tell anyone that I was leaving, where I was going, when I'd be back, because I didn't know myself. I saw the entire West through the windshield at seventy miles an hour, seen it bending past me and receding slowly in the rear-view mirror. The misty coast all the way to Portland, the volcanic Cascades, farm towns with new and used tractor lots instead of car lots. I'd become bored with the highway and turn off, one time finding myself on a marijuana plantation in Humboldt County, old rusted tractors and trucks placed carefully to give the impression of a logging camp, the distant barking and yelping of hounds cutting between densely packed trees. The interstates, the crumbling county roads, every winding dike road in the Delta. And as long as I was moving everything was fine. As long as the mural outside the windshield was changing, as long as the dashes on the road slipped beneath the left-front tire, I was OK. But whenever I stopped, whether it was for food or gas, or whether it was at a dead end dirt road in the farmlands, great fields of grain or vegetables fanning out and disappearing into horizon—no matter where or when I turned off the key and listened to the engine diesel a few times before coming to rest, it was always as if I had never been moving at all. Nothing had changed, nothing had gotten any better. I always feared that the car wouldn't start back up, that I'd be stuck wherever I was for the rest of my life, get murdered by some half-witted farmboy or lumberjack. But the car always did start, and I always got moving again, faster and faster, as if I were escaping from some invisible demon that always knew just where I was heading and would be waiting for me when I got there.

My flat has no furniture, only a single mattress I found next to a dumpster and a ghetto-blaster I bought long ago. As I write this essay, a cassette tape featuring Miles Davis's *Kind of Blue* and John Coltrane's *Blue Train* plays over and over, reminding me of the days before I was corrupted by the disease of Aesthetics, the days when only passion and the endless succession of primal screams constituted Being, the days before I read my first novel, when I was a trumpet player travelling the West with Mexican bands playing cumbias and rancheras and salsa, always the only gringo in the band. The walls of my flat are white, streaked with dried stains of moisture, remnants of sweltering East Bay Summer days—the curtains are thick and heavy. The floor is wood-float finished concrete, tiny ripples and streaks swirling beneath the feet, the traces of calloused hands gripping the tools of the mason. Sunrises and sunsets the walls and floor turn orange, gray rainy days, off-white when there's fog. Toilet's down the hall. I never cook, and therefore I don't need a stove or a woman. I've lived in my Oakland flat for two years now, the longest I've ever lived in one place, long enough for ex-girlfriends and creditors and relatives to find out where I am, but I still haven't hooked up a phone. I refuse to admit that live here. Habitat is a temporary condition. I'd still like to think that I'm only overlooking a dead-end temporarily, that the roar of the freeway interchange and the toasted chemical odor of the air are sociological specimens, fictions that I intend to write about someday, labors to endure—material for a novel that I'll never write. I prefer to think of my quarters as a kind of window-laboratory from which I study lower life-forms.

My window overlooks the end of a dead-end street, second floor, people above and below. There used to be a flashing light on a wooden pole to warn cars at night of the steel barrier. But drunks are drawn to flashing lights. The city of Oakland replaced the light twice before they gave up. The last person to ram into the barrier was my brother Clyde. He's dead now.

We had been talking about our crazy mother (she has 55 personalities and lives in a nut-house somewhere in Texas) and finishing the second liter of Chivas. There are some cheap things one can tolerate—Dutch Masters cigars, generic macaroni and cheese, women, Richland cigarettes—Scotch is not one of these things.

We got in a fight about something and he kicked my chest with his steel-toed work boots, broke three of my ribs. He didn't drink the fresh Chivas I poured him. He got up and left when I told him I was going to kill him.

I drank his drink after I finished the one I'd poured for myself. I didn't hear his car hit the pole at the end of the dead end. Nobody else must have either, because when I got up in the morning, many hours later, I saw the two tow trucks dragging out the wreckage, the medics bundling him up. The city sawed off the light pole at the base. Wrecks are more frequent, now, but less severe.

Past the dead end fourteen sets of railroad track string across the ground, some smooth and brilliant in summer noontime sun, most rusted and coarse beneath a bare foot. Old rotting railroad ties, eaten away by decades of rains and winter storms, countless loaded cars rhythmically pounding their weight down on the thick dark wood, driving it against the gravel, forcing it into the earth. The pulse of the Chinese immigrant, the black shipbuilder, the pulse of the executive, the boss, the rhythm of work, the time of jazz, the sweat of rhythm, the tracks they give, the tracks bend and bend, and just before they break there's less cars to run, and no one needs them now, and now they rust. Beyond, the Port of Oakland, its cargo cranes dominating the rim of the bay like immense girdered robots, slowly moving back and forth over ships, lifting, releasing. Trucks and ships and trains, cargo cranes and steel, smoke issuing steady and insistent, dispersing into the fog and clouds, steam rising across the railroad tracks, pumping and pumping, hanging thickly outside my flat's window, coloring my walls.

At night the bay is a black velvet cloth, shimmering as if speckled with the sequins of a giant bellydancer.

The asphalt street is no longer black, rather it is colorless and shiny, an ancient hazy mirror, frosted and webbed with tiny fractures. In the street a child stands watching black windows. A three legged collie hop-hops toward him two legs in the back one in the front. The child sees the collie coming, calls him, here boy, here boy. But the dog knows this boy. It has played with him before. The boy has held the bread above the collie's snout and circled the dog, and he has made the dog hop in a slow circle on his sturdy forepaw. They stand looking at each other, the dog strong on his tripod, the boy legs spread, ready for the showdown.

Summers the ice-cream man stops at the end of the dead end. He is a bearded man, thin and greasy, hair tied in a pony-tail. He always wears the same purple and yellow tie-dye shirt. He has never spoken a word to any of the swarming children. They pay and he hands over sidewalk sundaes and ice-cream sandwiches in silence. In a blaring tin-foil screech comes the music that announces his approach and arrival.

Wild geese that fly with the moon on their wings,

These are a few of my favorite things.

Stand at the iron barrier at the dead end and look away from the railroad and the port. Look at what you see. No matter what time of day the view looks like a withered black and white photograph. Clothes droop from the nylon stringers like gutted fish gathering soot and exhaust from freeways and factories. Porches and weed-strewn lawns, cars without shine, dull windshields, tar-shingled roofs peeling, a crushed paper 7-11 coffee cup settled next to the curb. You see California plates, Oakland A's bumper stickers, TV-20 KTVU, KFRC Plays the Hits, a pale styrofoam Union 76 ball on a car antenna. And it continues, it goes on as far as you can see. The street even seems to bend downward in the distance, it's as if you can see the curve of the earth. The street is endless, rippling and cracking. If you had a giant stick you'd run it against the houses like a kid runs a stick against a picket fence. The sound it would make would be like the shuffle of a deck of tired over-used playing cards. And you'd keep running that giant stick against the houses, feeling the rippling against your palm. And when you look back to see where you've been, you can't see the dead end anymore, nor any of the houses. There is a cloud of dust coming at you, rolling toward you, filling the street, swelling into the sky. You want to drop your stick, ditch the fucker and run, but you don't. You just stand there and let the dust come. You stand there and let it come.

This is what it's like on the street where I live. It's like this because I am a writer. Someone else might see it differently.

I am an educated academic writer. I confess. After seven years of college it's hard to not pull the theoretical pud of academia, to not write with the critics of the future in mind. I see no point in lying to you, leading you to believe that I'm operating in a literary vacuum, that I am not a writer surrounded by scores of used paperback books and any semblance of culture I can gather—monetarily or otherwise. If you are a person who has not labored through the great literature of the ages, if you are a truck driver or a Management Information Systems specialist or a Safeway-novel housewife following the life and times of some soap-opera couple, then this indulgent rant is not for you and I apologize if you have purchased it with your beer or lottery-ticket money. And what, then, should I make of this work? Should I use collage? Montage? Should I splatter the pages with contemporary references and leave the Norton Anthologists something to footnote? How about some theory that contradicts my journal entries? Or a structure that parallels the structure of a novelest's novel I may have read? Should I give the Ph.D. candidates something to research in their dissertations? How about some Joycean diarrhea for the workhogs to decipher and present at their next MLA conference? Was I really smoking three packs a day and drinking a liter of Scotch, filling my academic wastepaper basket with the burned-out butt-ends of my days and ways and the drunken dregs of a chemically induced imagination? How can I not think of these things? And how can one be so naive as to imagine that all post-Aristotelian artists were not thinking the same thing? If you see a parallel, dear workhog, it's there on purpose. I too have been corrupted by the history of my craft and by the institution of Aesthetics. And there is, mind you, nothing more crippling than the institution of Aesthetics, nothing that can destroy the bliss of indifference—and it is only through indifference, passionate homicidal entrail-ripping indifference, that Art can swell up like an encephalletic balloon and burst into being—like a program of aesthetic values. But aesthetics, however, does not belong to Art, it does not jive with my scotch and my cigatettes.

Aesthetics belongs to Associate Professor Einfache, to Professor Emeritus McKwiddit, to Professor Swineherd and Professor Dipshit.

Aesthetics is worth about twenty-five thousand dollars a year plus benefits.

Aesthetics reads papers at conferences in hopes of getting into *Modern*

Language Notes.

Aesthetics burns my asshole like Texas chile.

Aesthetics is the film of crud in my eyes when I wake up hungover in the afternoon.

Aesthetics is a herd of spirochetes stampeding through the veins of Art.

I spend my time reading novels, history, philosophy, and, when I am feeling especially generous with my time, even modern poetry. I watch public television, I go to museums, I try not to secure gainful employment, and although I sympathize with the uneducated class, I am not a member of its ranks. I attended the university, I ate macaroni and cheese and various dried bean concoctions for nearly ten years, I am not a milkman, a postal worker, a cab driver, a ditchdigger. Indeed, I've delivered newspapers, I've poured concrete, I've scrubbed the coffee stains from bosses' mohogany desks, from plush white carpet, I've had my skin burned off by hot tar and asphalt, I've manufactured health-food, I've built freeway overpasses, I've mixed drinks at seedy bars and at bars where I had to wear their starched uni-colored uniform. I was a caretaker, Pinter-style, in Marin County, watching over private tennis courts, protecting nylon nets from theft in the night.

I have finished the concrete slabs your glass and steel building rests upon.

I've done the shit work, the work the fat-faced red-neck whiskey-gutted blue-collar grunt has done. I've watched seven men die on construction sites, seen men flopping on the ground like fish in the dirt, their pants fouled, seen men with their skulls split and splattered like hammer-beaten watermelons, seen the way the corpses' eyes clouded and ceased to see. I've passed out from exhaustion before lunchtime. But I'm not one of them, I never have been, and I hereby declare it, unabashedly, without reservation, without guilt. You see, I'm not a postal worker, I'm not a milkman, and as poor as I might be, as little money I might have to spend on VCR's and wristwatch-televisions and ice-making refrigerators, I still haven't become one of the bucket-headed middle-class television-stupored clots of ignorance that today's writers claim to be and fraternally embrace. In my fiction, the first person, the "I" of my narrative, is the most important character. The occasional "you" is an implication, a chastisement, an insult. I don't want to hear about your pain, I refuse to listen to your laments: I've howled myself and I have no sympathy. Eat your own excrement. I didn't do it. I've looked out of my window at night and seen the smog, I've breathed the same shit in the air that you have, I've walked out my door at three in the morning and smelled the stench of the great American armpit. I know it's there, and I don't claim to embrace it. I condemn it. And I condemn you.

But don't get me wrong—I'm not without compassion. If I had no compassion for the human condition I wouldn't bother to write, I'd sit in a crowded dark hovel and laugh, laugh like a deathly complacent green-faced ghoul in an amusement park haunted house at the ridiculousness of your plight, your woeful eternal suffering. My compassion has nearly ruined me, and it is only by objectifying that compassion that I can utter a single syllable. Perhaps it's the human condition as an abstraction that I sympathize with rather than the individual man. I can know the abstraction because I am part of it, but the only individual man I know is T-Bird Murphy. So I'm not going to tell you the story of a plumber who has left his plunger on the job and finds an analogy between the plunger and God, or a story about a bored housewife, a preacher's wife, a jealous wife, a midwife, an ex-wife, etc. I'm not going to waste my time writing about a professional lawnmower whose blades are stuck and therefore contemplates the origins of the cosmos. I've got better things to write about—like myself.

Not so many years ago, when I first began writing, I wanted to grab the testicles of the great dick of humanity and squeeze until it screamed, then squeeze some more. I wanted to sing the song of the downtrodden working class, the oppressed minorities, the millions of people who have lost control of their miserable destinies. I wanted to change the world. I saw myself as a teenaged visionary, a prophet, a man who saw more in the world than everyone else did, and I saw it as my calling to open their crusted eyes. I didn't see the world as the mindless, peaceful Seine, flowing ceaselessly through the hills and cities to the ocean. Its course may have been fixed, I thought, but it was the Nimitz freeway at five o'clock, the Jersey Turnpike at rush hour, it was the sewage canal that ran silently beneath us all, rotting, stinking, festering, but always ignored, put out of sight and mind. I wanted to dig up the streets, to uncover the sewers, to let the people see what they were made of. Just because they hadn't looked between their legs before they flushed didn't mean that I intended to let them get away with not taking a chomp out of the fruit of the tree. I was going to leave the torn up streets wide and gaping like a great whore's worm-eaten cunt, and I wanted everyone to fall in, and when they finally smelled the stench, they would know that they were alive. I was tired of happy endings, and I wanted someone to show one to me so that I could laugh in his face and spit on the last page of his manuscript.

Of course I was young and foolish then. I didn't know that my song had been sung before. I didn't realize the folly of my young taut gonads. My friends and neighbors loved my writing, and I didn't realize that the worst indicator of the worth of writing is universal approval, which is the resultant opinion when a work does no more than reinforce preconceived notions. If you want everyone to like your work, just say what they've already said themselves. I didn't know I was a silly ass, that people are downtrodden because they choose to be so, that our great slums and sprawling ghettos and grease soaked tenements are perhaps the greatest achievements of our country, the freest domains the human animal can inhabit. Where I live, in my flat overlooking the dead end and Oakland,

I am more free than I have ever been. If I want to break windows like I did as a boy just two miles from here, if I want to lay blubbering in the gutter drunk or stoned or frying on hallucinogens, if I want to starve myself and sit decomposing in a heap of academic residue, if I want to stand on the cracking concrete floor and howl like Ivan Ilyich for days on end—anything I want to do I can do, and no one will bother me, no one will interrupt my life. I have never spoken with my neighbors—haven't even tried.

The morning I walked out onto my porch and watched the sun come up, watched it rise into the fogless day like a great white ulcer, an ulcer that seemed to be both etched into the heavens and etched into my soul, it took me a long time to do anything but think and smoke cigarettes and try to heal the ulcer. But the wound wouldn't heal. The more I thought the more it opened. The sun became brighter and brighter, and as its intensity increased, as the shadows darkened and stretched across the city, as the dirty windows blazed like mirrors and burned my eyes, the ulcer grew and seemed to be a condensed sun ready to explode in my chest, or as Beowulf would have said, eager to burst my heart-coffin. I'd never before seen Oakland or the bay or San Francisco lit from the East. Whenever I'd had the chance before, I had always been lying in bed awake or on the freeway or on a jobsite submerged in the bowels of the city, below the water table, below the asphalt and concrete crust of the earth, and I'd never considered anything more than my current distraction. I'd always seen the buildings and the wires and the telephone poles from beneath the noonday sun or scattered through the afternoon and dinnertime fog and haze as if refracted through a celestial smokestack prism. I clenched my fists in front of my face and squeezed my eyes shut. When I opened my eyes, I looked through the space between my fists as if looking through a telescope, and I thought about what I needed, what was missing, how, if possible, I could remain a man and not revert back into the compost pile of erudition I'd become. And what I wanted to do, I realized, was something that wouldn't be the same as something I'd read in a novel—I wanted to live a new plot, speak sentences no one had written before, I wanted meet people who weren't characters in Chekhov's short stories, women who weren't poets' muses or Faulkner's whores and bossy old hags, men who I could talk with and drink beer with and range the country with and at the same time who I could not place in a text I had read before taking my Code 64 GRE's or comprehensive exams. But I feared that it was impossible, that I'd been corrupted to a life of novelistic comparison. I feared that I was condemned to see people as characters, characters to be compared and contrasted with any of the thousands of characters I'd memorized for identification questions.

When a person reads too much, when he lives many vicarious lives in a short space of time, he becomes old when he is very young. I tried to think of something I could do that I had not read about, something I could do and not feel like my life was one plagiarized scene after another, and I could think of nothing.

I walked down the stairs and into the street, stood at the iron barrier at the end of the dead end and felt the gravel beneath my bare feet. The sensation was queer, almost vertiginous, the way my skin conformed to the contours of the earth, the way I could feel the air hugging my clothes and my exposed skin. I could feel the pulse of the planet wrapping me and nursing me, and I felt nothing sinister, no demon or god; rather I felt as if I were being invited into a world that had been waiting for me to have the consciousness to comprehend. I had an impulse to dash back up to the john in my flat and finish Proust. But I resisted the impulse to finish the book, and I remained on the street, looking at the city from ground level instead of from two stories above. I had not often left my apartment since I moved in two years before—I had had no need to work because I had saved a good deal of money from doing construction, and for the first year, I received bi-monthly unemployment checks from the generous State of California Treasury. In the beginning I had walked the streets often, but the occasions became less and less frequent, and the less frequent my expeditions became, the odder I felt, the more out of place I seemed to be. The Victorian houses, the shops, the sidewalk and the battered cars and graffiti-walls of the stores seemed less real, more phantasmagorical, more like an urban scene from *Call it Sleep* or *Berlin Alexanderplatz*. The more I read the less I found a need to see the world myself—the world of fiction was far more real and infinitely more revealing than anything I could sense myself. And I wondered if there were anything left for me to do. I was certain that there was nothing to write about, and that didn't bother me, as long ago I had given up the hope, and more importantly the desire, that I could further clutter the overburdened Dewey Decimal system with another card-catalogue number. I had already resolved to be a writer of the mind instead of a writer of the pen. What bothered me was that I felt more like a character in a poorly written novel than like a man of flesh and bone.

I would have done nothing if I hadn't turned back and read the graffiti and the bumper-stickers again. I would have dropped my head, walked backed into my flat and shut my eyes, or perhaps picked up a book of criticism. But instead I noticed a child, the child who usually teased the three-legged collie, spraying on the wood-slat wall of Pete's Market and Liquors. Pete is a small thin Chinese man who owns the market and sprays the urine and the cigarette butts out of the doorway and into the gutter each morning at eleven when he opens the store. On Pete's light green wall, the child wrote, "FUCK YOU," and when he stepped back to look at his handicraft, he did not consider the history of the phrase, how many times it had been uttered and inscribed, the Nobel Prize winners who had used the words at precisely the perfect juncture in their tales, he did not paint over his words and revise them and step back and reconsider his revision: rather, he crossed his arms over his small thin chest and saw that it was good.

I turned back to my apartment and looked at it, looked at the sagging roof and the peeling shingles, the blood-like rust stains beneath the rain gutters streaking the dull white paint as if the building had been suffering from an ancient wound and had been steadily bleeding ever since. And I knew that to escape the bondage of Aesthetics I would have to leave this place, that I would have to once again get into my car and drive, leave my books and pens and postcards and paper behind and live my own version of the Great American Stereotype. I went back into my flat and closed A la recherche du temps perdu and lay down in the middle of the floor, my back heavy against the cool concrete floor, and I sighed a very deep sigh.

I did not adhere to my resolution. When I finally had my car packed the back seat was piled with books, every book it would hold. I had intended only to bring the best, the writers who inspired me the most, the visionaries of my academic memories, writers who had changed my perception of the world. Not very often does one meet a person who, when he is speaking to you, says something so profound, so poetic, so beautiful, a person whose words quake your soul so deeply, that you ask him to repeat his words, to re-speak what he has said so that you might attempt to assimilate those words into your very consciousness. More likely, a speaker's words enter the air and disintegrate into the backdrop of the noise of the universe, no more distinct than the hiss and crackle of interstellar dust. How many of us ever get a chance to be a Plato and hear the words of a Socrates? or a Boswell with Johnson? St. Mark and Jesus Christ esq.? Today, it seems, we can only be shaken by the words in books. There are only paper prophets. I began by merely packing a Gideon's Bible, intending to read through the book and steal quotes for later use. But then I decided that if I were going to take a Bible, I might as well take Proust. What a treat it would be to read the book in the context of freedom and motion, in a distant field or hotel room or woman's house, rather than in stagnation, mildew, and my sagging Oakland ceiling! And after I allowed myself this luxury, I took *Moby Dick* from the shelf. Then I tossed in *Ulysses* and the *Odyssey*, and then *Paradise Lost*, and my Riverside Shakespeare and Kafka's journals, Poe's tales and Balzac, Wallace Stevens and Whitman, *Tom Jones* and Dante, Beckett, Faulkner, Aeschylus and Euripides and *Three Trapped Tigers*, Cormac McCarthy's *Blood Meridian* and *Suttree*, and the box was full, and I needed more boxes, and the back seat of my car was packed tight and I put my clothes in the trunk.

My migration, I decided, was to be eastward. I'd grown up in the Bay Area, been spawned in the breeding pools of the early sixties, I'd spent my time living in the sumptank of urban California, the mockery of every New York Jew and Bostonian prig I'd ever read or come across. I grew up, as Henry James said, "in America, in Texas, in Nebraska, in California or somewhere—somewhere that scarcely counted as a definite place at all; it showed somehow, from afar, as so lost, so indistinct and illusory, in the great alkali desert of cheap Divorce." The Oakland ghettos I grew up in, the gunfights between Mexican low-rider gangs at my high school, and the acid and quaaludes and crystal that killed my brother Owen when he was thirteen, the black children beaten daily to death by their overburdened parents—these were the products of the so-called land of sit-coms, of *Gilligan's Island*, of Soap-Opera love, of *Three's Company* and every low-budget police-drama the writers could scrape out of the bowls of their hash pipes and hookahs and bhongs. The writers's happy cops always had a handicap—Cannon's was that he was extremely fat; Ironsides chased down crooks in his wheelchair; Barnaby Jones was always on the verge of having a coronary arrest; McCloud was surgically attached to his cowboy hat. I was supposedly as bad off as the California-studio-produced TV cops—my handicap, I was repeatedly informed through literature, by professors, by every pompous column writer in the Sunday

Times, was that I was a barbaric Californian, and as a barbaric Californian had had the mistaken notion that San Francisco and Los Angeles and Seattle were cities like other cities, cities with roaches in the kitchens and muggers in the parks. According to the easterners I was a foolish simpleton because I thought that New York was no more than a San Francisco with Puerto Ricans and Italians instead of Mexicans and Chinese, and when I either grew up or took a crash course on being civilized I would certainly understand that New York and the rest of the East is the glowing zenith of the intellectual and urban eternity. How could I be so ignorant as to think that we California folk, riding around in our four-wheel-drive pickup trucks and wearing holsters and chaps and ten-gallon Stetsons and singing the disco version of the national anthem, have any real problems? How could I have the gall to think that I, an offspring of that great alkali desert, could become an intellectual, let alone a writer, if I had not spent the greater part of my days in New York City, or Poughkeepsie perhaps?

Before I had loaded the car and packed in all my books, I'd been resolved to remain a writer of the mind, but now, as my indignation grew and I felt myself teetering on the verge of voyage, the writer of the pen began to rise once again. I saw myself travelling across the great Nevada wasteland, over the Rockies and into the plains, I saw myself stopping at small towns and truckstops and hick villages in Nebraska and Kansas, and I imagined all of the character sketches I would be able to draw, the descriptions of terrain and medieval tribes in the prehistoric states of Texas, Kentucky (does Kentucky even have a city?), Wyoming; I imagined stopping at bookstores and buying hand-bound journals in which I would record my no doubt stunning sociological and geological observations. I was going to show the New Yorkers and the Parisians and the Londoners and the Dubliners that it was possible to, as Ferlinghetti would say, Start from San Francisco, that Chinese-built railroad tracks were hammered into the earth with the same sweat and dreams as Irish tracks, that Harlem is but a sister of Watts and West Oakland, that the Brooklyn Bridge and the Golden Gate are kindred souls. But, in the height of this reverie, I stopped and clenched my teeth and I looked back out over the bay, over the factories and warehouses and freeways and tenements—and I realized that I was back where I'd started, living the bloodsuck life of the lowest form of literary parasite, ready once again to bind myself between the covers of a rambling narrative, ready to dispatch my soul and live for The Text. I had come full circle, and was dangerously close to negating my epiphany of the night before and canceling it out into the null of syllogistic academic suit-and-tie oblivion.

I quickly unloaded the books—hauled them back up the stairs and into my flat. Then I unloaded the rest of the car, unpacked the provisions I had so carefully tucked beneath the spare tire, under the seats, in the trunk. I opened the glove compartment and took out the road maps and threw them in the dumpster across the street.

I turned the key and felt the low rumble of the engine, the steady massage of pistons and valves, heard the sound of air being sucked into the carburetor, the fan flooding the engine with a stream of dusk. The dashboard clock showed six o'clock. Across the street I could see the boy who had painted "FUCK YOU" on the side-wall of Pete's Market. He was sitting on the curb eating a sandwich and looking at his inscription.

I drove.

Kickshaws

—Hey we got a letter but on the envelope it says don't open it should we.

—Who's it addressed to.

—Occupant.

—It's for you. I never get letters.

—No. You don't. That's what you get for writing so many. Who wants to answer a letter when they know they're going to get one right back it's a nuisance.

(Pause)

—Either it's raining or it's not raining what's a man to do.

—If you lay on your back in the dark you might see things differently.

—Doesn't work.

—Sometimes I give the objects in the room Anglo-Saxon names works wonders or maybe start a crustacean collection.

—Tried it.

—You've tried everything.

—Yes and it all reduces to tautologies and hepatoscopy.

—What about what's her name.

—Strictly vegetarian. There's a difference between trying and succeeding one way you fail and the other way you don't accomplish anything.

—Look it's raining.

—See. I'm right.

&

—Could be a letter bomb playing on our instinctual desire for knowledge of the unknown. Could be a sweepstakes prize and if we open it we lose the prize. Could be some crap from your brother Herbert.

(Pause)

—You mean Harold.

—No I mean Herbert you said your brother's name was Herbert I heard you.

(Pause)

—Did I.

—Certainly.

—Okay I take your word for it what do you think Harold has to say maybe changed his name and doesn't want the authorities to know.

—Could be retaliation. For the letters I've been sending.

(Pause)

—You never told me about letters what letters.

—Nothing. Never mind. Look it's not raining now and I'm right again. It's boring being right so often. Maybe it's just some kind of joke. You know. A prank played by some malicious gastroenterologist.

—That settles it my brother Harold is a gastroenterologist. Therefore it must be from him.

(Pause)

—You don't want to know about the letters I've been sending.

—No.

(Pause)

—But you did before.

—Wrong.

(Pause)

—Sounded like you did.

(Pause)

—Phone's ringing.

—Not my job to answer the phone. You know the rules.

—Okay, I'll answer it like a dutiful servant. I'm a man who plays by the rules…. It's for you.

&

—Well.

—Recorded message. He played a Charlie Parker tune on a throat warbler.

—What did he say.

(Pause)

—Said open the letter.

&

—Aren't you going to answer the letter it's your letter.

—But I haven't opened it I don't know who it's from I don't know if he'll ever get my answer.

—Sure he'll get it who do you think gets all those Dear Santa letters those Dear Congressman letters those Dear Jahweh letters those Dear Herbert letters. He'll get it all right. Might even be a she this could be a change in your life never know. Come on open the letter.

—Okay I'll open the letter I know you sent it anyway.

&

—Well.

 —It's a blank piece of thesis bond.

 —No it's not I'm sure there's writing on it I know.

 —Wrong. Blank. Nothing.

 —But.

 —I think it's Mallarme's *Le Livre*.

 —But.

 —Zip. Postmodern to the max.

&

—How's the weather doing.

 —Fog, baby. Fog.

Wamsutter in Dali Vision

"That's one thing about the West, Johnny Boy, they don't have dead bodies over a hundred years old there," Brent Holingsworth said. He flicked an ash in his newly stolen MGM Grand ashtray.

"You've got a point there," Johnny Staples said. "In California our dead bodies aren't very old."

The Wamsutter Wyoming Super 8 motor hotel television was not operating nearly as well as a New York television or even as well as a San Francisco television. Brent and Johnny wondered if the television in room 129, the room next door, was any better than theirs. *Dobie Gillis* was on. *Dobie Gillis* in Dali Vision. Johnny too lit up a Merit Light, and in alternating reaches, together with Brent flicked his ashes in the ashtray which was to be the newest addition to their array of stolen furniture in their apartment in Boulder, Colorado.

&

In room 129, the two other travelers, Axel and Ruth Gleibenheim were having a worship session. This was abundantly evident, not only because of blatant foreshadowing, but because of compounding evidence which could not be denied by either Johnny nor Brent.

&

It had been sixty hours since they had left San Francisco. Sixty hours together in a Volkswagen Beetle, no stereo, no tire chains, no U.S. currency. Ruth was hungry again. It was still sixty miles across a sheet of ice until they would reach the next hotel. It was three o'clock already, and they were only going twenty miles per hour. Johnny would not stop the car for food. "We'll never make it alive if we don't find a place to stop before dark," Johnny said. Brent snickered and agreed.

Ruth

whined
claimed she had to pee again
held her stomach
whispered to Axel
watched snowdrift buried billboards
whined.

&

Johnny's grandparents were tired after working all day to prepare Thanksgiving dinner. Johnny had brought along his roommate from New York, Brent Holingsworth, and the couple which managed the Ford Apartments back in Boulder, Axel and Ruth Gleibenheim. Axel Gleibenheim painted oil portraits of thin women with large breasts. Ruth's breasts were only average in size. Axel was thinking of how large Johnny's stepmother's breasts were, and how much he would like to see what her nipples looked like. He wanted to paint those breasts. Ruth was watching Johnny's little brother, who had just completed his first Pacific cruise with the Navy on the USS Berkeley. She was wishing that Axel had a little more meat on him, though she still didn't like tattoos.

&

Axel sat with the group of artists in the Boulderado lounge, discussing perspective and the lithograph procedure that Dali used in his "Lincoln in Dali Vision" painting. "It's so simple, yet so complicated," he said. The others nodded and sipped their drinks.

"What time are we leaving for San Francisco?" Ruth whispered into Johnny's ear. "I can hardly wait." She leaned over and nibbled on Johnny's ear, then inserted her tongue and twirled.

Johnny was uncomfortable. He looked down from the counter he and Ruth were sitting on at the table where Axel and the other art critics were sitting. He wanted Ruth to retract her tongue, but he didn't ask her to stop.

"When you look at the painting, at first it looks like a woman standing in front of a window that is shaped like a cross," Axel said. "But if you look again, you can see Lincoln's face in it."

"Lincoln's face?" one asked.

"With the beard?" asked another.

"Yes," Axel replied. "With the beard."

&

Ruth had to go to pee. The travelers had been trapped in a traffic jam at 6000 feet for seven hours, just west of Donner Pass. They sat in the car watching taillights. The snow was piled high on the hood of the Volkswagen. "I wish I was a man," Ruth said.

"I'm glad I am," Brent said, and he got out of the car and disappeared into the snow and trees.

Ruth

whined
looked out at the trees
squirmed
thought about men with meat on them
whined.

"Let me out," Ruth told Brent when he, relieved, returned. "Come on, Axel, come with me. I don't want to get attacked."

"You'll be OK honey."

"Come with me."

"She's leaning on my car, dammit," Johnny said, as he and Brent watched. Axel was standing by, protecting against possible assailants in the six-inch-per-hour snowstorm. But Axel had neglected to hold Ruth up, and Ruth had underestimated the slipperyness of the ice.

"Difficult footing," Brent noted.

Johnny agreed.

&

Besides being severely distorted in both color and shape, Dobie Gillis was having problems. Maynard had accidentally swallowed a serum which made him irresistible to women, and Dobie's girlfriend had left him for Maynard.

In room 129 the worship session continued.

In room 128 Johnny and Brent wished they had marijuana. They also wished that they had enough money for some food.

"We'll never make it back alive," Johnny said.

&

Grandfather Staples watched Johnny and his friends from college in Colorado as they finished up their Thanksgiving dinners. They were amazed with Ruth. They had never before seen a woman who did not help with dishes.

Grandmother Staples whispered to Grandfather Staples: "I've never before seen a woman who did not help with the dishes."

Grandfather Staples nodded.

&

Johnny woke up and looked out the front window of the Volkswagen. All he saw was white. Have they started letting cars over the pass yet? he wondered. He looked through the side window and saw another car, and then looked at his watch. Ten hours lost already. He looked at Brent. Sleeping as usual. He looked in the rear view mirror and saw Axel, but he could not see Ruth. He could, however, hear Ruth. He saw that Axel was smiling and breathing heavily, his eyes closed. A worship session, Johnny thought, and looked back at the white windshield and thought about how nice it would be if he were asleep.

&

The travelers were somewhere in Utah, between Wendover Nevada and Salt Lake City. Ruth and Brent were in the back seat, sleeping. Axel was driving and Johnny was in charge of keeping him awake and supplying him with fresh beers.

"Sure is a wonderful lady I've found myself, that Ruth," Axel said. "Don't you think so, Johnny?"

"Wonderful lady, Axel."

Axel was not watching the road. He was looking at Johnny.

Johnny looked away, out the windshield. A lot of ice on the road, Johnny noted. Good thing that the engine is over the drive wheels on Volkswagens.

Axel looked at the road, then back at Johnny. "I'd sure hate to lose her. I don't know what I'd do without her."

"Would you like to take a break?" Johnny asked. "I'll drive if you're tired."

"No. I'll drive." Axel looked at the road again. "You just ride," he said.

&

The television was still on in the Wamsutter Super 8, and now David Hartman was suffering distortion on Good Morning America. America is the most overfed country in the world, his guest was saying.

Johnny woke up first and turned off the television. He looked over at Brent, and was happy that Brent didn't snore. "Get up," Johnny said. "It's time to get moving."

In the car, Axel and Ruth were more than happy to take the back seat.

"Let's stop and get some breakfast," Ruth said. "I'm famished."
"But we don't have any money," Johnny said.
"Just put it on your credit card, and we'll pay you back later."
"But you and Axel have credit cards, and so does Brent."
"I just thought it would be simpler. We've been using yours all along."
"Yes, we have," Johnny said.

Johnny

scowled
watched the ice on the road
thought about the overturned trucks he had seen
wished he had a car stereo
wondered how much Wyoming French Toast cost
scowled.

"Now aren't you glad you stopped for breakfast, Johnny?" Ruth asked. "What a lovely little cafe. Aren't you glad?"

The hostess/waitress/cook/cashier/tow-truck dispatcher brought the bill.

"Here's my three," Brent said.
"Been holding out on us, eh?" Axel said.

"And here's four and a half from me," Johnny said.

"But that leaves us paying nine twenty-five," Ruth said, aiming at Johnny.

"But you owe me fifteen," Johnny said.

"I thought I owed that to Brent?"

"No. To me."

"But how much was your meal?" she asked. "Who's going to get the tip?"

Johnny got up and went outside.

Johnny could not see through the fogged cafe window. Instead, he watched a man in a faded GMC half-ton tow-truck dragging around an old railroad tie with chains, trying to clear away some of the snow in the lot. It was not doing much good. The snow was piling up in front of the wood, then flowing over it and settling down again, in a new location, as deep as it had been in the first place.

Rhoda's Sack

Marvin Mitkowitz, Branch Manager of the accounting firm, is obsessed with the need to discover the contents of Rhoda's sack. He has never seen such an inappropriate piece of ladies' apparel in all his sixteen years of directing the affairs of the office. The utter ugliness of the dated hippyish hand-knit multicolored sack (perhaps not laundered since its original date of manufacture) hanging from her drooping shoulder each day when she sluggishly, apathetically, yet somehow haughtily enters the office gives him more than a slight feeling of uneasiness, of revulsion, of intense, almost pathological (he is aware of this) curiosity.

Will it disintegrate some morning on her way to work, the contents spilling on the sidewalk for all to see? And if it does, can he somehow manage to be there at the moment of incident?

Is this her way, subversive as it seems, of asking for a raise?

Rhoda Gleibenheim, the second-cousin of Marvin Mitkowitz's immediate superior in the main office, knows many things. She knows what the neighbors, sleeping in their flats, are dreaming about while she, Rhoda, slaves away at the typewriters and wordprocessors in the office. She knows what the bus driver looks at when each morning she, wearing the most modest of wool sweaters, ascends the steps (which are altogether too steep for her severely overworked legs), withdraws her mittened hand from her sack, and deposits her hard-earned quarters. She knows the lurid minds of her colleagues. She knows what they think when each morning she walks into the office and pours herself a cup of coffee into her Magic-Marker monogrammed Styrofoam cup. She knows her spelling and grammatical rules: i *before* e except after *c*; occasion without an *ai*; s-e-p-*a-r*-a-t-e. She knows her it's/its. Marvin Mitkowitz, she knows, cannot do without her.

Rhoda deserves a raise.

Marvin carefully lights cigarette #6 and observes the clock, which reads 9:13, then fixes his gaze on the frosted glass door entrance. He knows that her bus arrives at 9:03 at the corner two blocks away, and it takes her anywhere from 10 to 20 minutes to walk the distance, depending on the perils she must brave on the city's crowded sidewalks. But though he is aware of the reasons behind her daily tardiness, he has never become accustomed to allowing employees to be consistently, insistently, uncompromisingly late. What, he wonders, is the impact on the other employees' morale? What do they think of him, Branch Manager, tolerating such blatant insolence?

What is this power she has over him?

He carefully lights cigarette #7. He studies the entrance.

It is 9:12 and Rhoda has been standing across the street for nearly ten minutes now, persistently tapping her aged worn shoe on the sidewalk. From her vantage point, she can see the second-story office window as clearly as she does on any other morning. She can see his big comfy leather chair swiveling nervously back and forth, though his head swings with perfect timing in the opposite direction, thereby allowing him to keep his gaze fixed on the entrance which she has no intention whatsoever of passing through for at least another ten minutes. She can see the cloud of cigarette smoke lifting up over his balding head.

She'll get her money's worth out of him one way or another.

And he knows what she'll do when she prances through the frosted glass door. He's seen her perform her routine every working day for the past year. He's seen her enter drowsily, lethargically, yet impertinently, keeping her shabby tweed coat pulled tightly over her wool-sweatered breasts, refusing to pull her hands out of her mittens and begin typing until her near-frostbitten fingers are sufficiently warmed and nimble. He's seen her pour coffee into her Magic Marker monogrammed Styrofoam cup and he knows that never, never, does she leave the contributory nickel that the other employees do toward the purchase of the next can of coffee. He's heard her talking with the accountants: *Isn't it cold in here to you? It's like the arctic. What's he think this is, a meat freezer? I have to walk miles in the cold, that's why I'm nearly half-dead. My car's in the shop, you know.* And each morning, Marvin Mitkowitz, as do the accountants, pretends that he does not hear Rhoda. But though he attempts to shut down his auditory system, he cannot do the same with his visual apparatus. His eyes, from the instant she prances through the frosted glass door, do not leave her ugly hand knit multicolored sack (perhaps not laundered since its original date of manufacture).

Marvin remembers his first encounter with Rhoda and her sack, the fateful day he interviewed her for the position his immediate superior (Rhoda's second-cousin) in the main office had personally recommended, if not requested, he appoint her to. She entered the office sluggishly, indiligently, yet somehow with an air of procacity, her short frame seeming to creak and moan like an old dead tree bending in the wind, her aging tattered sack on the verge of instantaneous and utter decomposition. Marvin sat in his big leather swiveling chair, smoking a cigarette, trying to ascertain the quality of the visible portion of her legs. There was not, however, much to examine, owing to the out-of-style length of her dress. And what there was to examine was not pleasant: in fact, the sight of her calves, white and swollen, the skin stretched much too tight over the tissue, spiderwebbing networks of blue and green veins (which, amazingly, did not protrude from the surface, but rather appeared as if traced on with tiring felt-tip pens), walnut-sized bruises splotching the skin, was to Marvin one of the most disagreeable spectacles he had bore witness to in many years.

What are you looking at? Rhoda said.

Nothing, Madam, Marvin said. He could not help but note the droning, whining, nasal quality of her voice.

Why should I work for you? Rhoda said. What benefits do you have to offer someone as talented as I?

Won't you take your mittens off and make yourself comfortable, Miss...

Rhoda, Rhoda said. Rhoda Gleibenheim. And no I will not take off my mittens, if you please. I do not wish to hamper the flow of blood to my fingertips by exposing them to the inappropriate chill of your office space. I have no intention of making myself susceptible to arthritis prematurely. No, Sir, I will not take off my mittens.

Certainly you will relieve yourself of your coat?

Certainly I will not.

If you are hired, Marvin said, you will find the working conditions quite agreeable.

Rhoda spoke: My car is in the shop, and I therefore will require more time than the other employees to arrive in the morning. Needless to say, it will also be necessary for me to depart considerably earlier than your other employees. Do you have a cigarette? she asked, putting her fingers over her lips for Marvin to reflect upon, in the event that he could not decipher her nasal string of morphemes.

Marvin Mitkowitz, who was not in the habit of lending cigarettes to anyone, neither bums who begged persistently for cigarettes, nor employees who never ventured to ask, for he brought exactly ten to the office each morning which he smoked one each hour on the hour, was taken aback by this sudden, unexpected request. A man of business, a man of finesse, a man capable of handling multi-million dollar accounts, a man able to handle his employees adroitly, skillfully, lucidly, if not forcefully, vigorously, (yet rarely unfairly,) Marvin had never before been faced with this dilemma: Rhoda, the prospective secretary (personally *recommended*, if not *requested* for employment by Marvin's immediate superior in the main office), lay somewhere between bum and employee, as Marvin had not yet the time to ascertain her relative position. For sixteen years he had smoked ten cigarettes, no more, no less, each hour on the hour during his workday. Were he to give her one of his cigarettes, which hour's allotment of tobacco would it be?

The woman was awaiting a response.

Not without reluctance, not without the most painful effort, not without the severest disinclination ever a man silently endured, did Marvin reach into his shirt-pocket and withdraw a cigarette, thereupon handing it to Rhoda, who received it with an open mitten.

Can I have *two*? Rhoda asked.

As Rhoda watches Marvin swiveling and smoking, clouding the office in nervous expectation (Rhoda is aware of this) of her tardy entrance, she thinks about how indispensable she has become around the office. And Rhoda has not expended a minimum of effort to secure this situation. Rhoda has hidden the coffee can where no one but her can find it. Rhoda periodically changes all the filenames on the hard-disk (not to mention the numerous floppys) so that none but her can make use of the computer. Rhoda has reorganized the contents of the eleven filing cabinets which still contain (Rhoda has not had the time yet to enter all of the data into the computer system) most of the company's important records: instead of being filed in the standard alphabetical manner, Rhoda has filed the documents alphabetically with respect to the second letter of the client's name: Bandy & Co under *A*, Ebbetson Associates under *B*, Acne Acoutrements under *C*, and so on. Only Rhoda possesses the knowledge needed to set the machinations of the office into motion each morning.

No day can begin until Rhoda opens the frosted glass door and passes through the office entrance.

Rhoda observes as Marvin, still swiveling, lights another cigarette.

Marvin considers the clock, which reads 9:23, and lights cigarette #8. With Fortune in his ranks, he'll be sucking away at #10, filling the clouded office with billows of sweet pale smoke (Marvin chortles to himself here), when she enters indifferently, phlegmatically, yet condescendingly nonchalant, as if she is cognizant (and he knows damned well she must be) of the power she and her sack hold over him. This accursed power has its origin in that first meeting when she took the second cigarette (the first dangling unlit between her plump, withered lips) from his leery hand and, with decisiveness and firm resolution, as well as a suspiciously well-rehearsed and skillfully practiced motion, deposited the prize into her dumpy shabby hand-knit sack (perhaps unlaunderable at all due to its tenuous composition).

After witnessing the adroitness and deftness Rhoda had employed inserting the second cigarette into her sack, Marvin could not help but wonder how many cigarettes the sack contained. Certainly he was not her first victim. Perhaps, he thought, the sack only contains my cigarette: but perhaps it contains hundreds, even thousands (judging by the way in which the sack bulged) of borrowed cigarettes, Pall Malls, Lucky Strikes, Merit Ultra-Lights, Camels, Scotch Buys, Dorals—who knows how many brand names? and how far back they might date? Perhaps she is collecting them in case of a wartime shortage. Marvin was seized with the desire to snatch her sack and examine the contents. Who knows what he might find?

I'll take the job, Rhoda said. I will start immediately, though I must remind you that I will be leaving considerably earlier than the other employees due to my transportation situation.

Marvin remembered how Rhoda perambulated through the office, scrutinizing the working conditions, shivering in protest though she was still wearing her coat and mittens, the sack slung over her drooping shoulder, bulging with his cigarette. She approached one of the employees.

Hi there, she said. Got a cigarette?

Rhoda did not look back at Marvin. She smiled a toothy smile at the employee.

Sure, the employee replied. Sure I've got a cigarette.

Thank you, Rhoda said upon receiving the cigarette. How about a dollar? You got a dollar I can have?

But the employee, upon seeing, out of the corner of his eye, his boss Marvin, who was shaking his head spasmodically in an effort to persuade his employee to give Rhoda a response in the negative, gave Rhoda a response in the negative.

No, he said. No I sure don't have a dollar.

Rhoda twirled the cigarette between her thumb and index and middle fingers like a drum-major manipulating a baton, then, adroitly and deftly, slipped the cigarette into her swelling sack.

I must, Marvin thinks, sitting in his swiveling leather boss's chair while attending to the clock, which now reads 9:28, see the inside of that sack!

Apathetically, Rhoda ascends the stairs, feeling especially weary today, not quite lethargic, but merely slightly drowsy. She stands outside the frosted glass door, watching her watch and wondering if she is being watched from within. She has exacted exactly thirty-two minutes of the company's due labor, which she multiplies by eleven, (the number of employees who have been standing idly by anticipating her entrance,) and computes the figure of 352 man-minutes of labor. She'll get her money's worth out of him one way or another.

Rhoda places her hand against the frosted glass and gives the door a firm, haughty shove.

When Rhoda enters, Marvin stops swiveling in his leather boss's chair. He has not yet finished cigarette #9, and therefore still has one left in his shirt-pocket. He sucks on the filter furiously in an attempt to smoke the cigarette all the way down to the butt; for, as he knows, if he leaves any tobacco in the paper, Rhoda will lift the butt from the ashtray and deposit it in her sack. However, if he has not yet begun cigarette #10, Rhoda will ask to borrow it. And how can he, Marvin Mitkowitz, Branch Manager, refuse her? On what grounds would he base the refusal? Certainly he draws a sturdy enough wage to be able to afford purchasing another pack if the cigarette he lends her happens to be his last. Certainly a cigarette, the twentieth part of a single dollar, is worth less than he has dropped in the gutter and decided too worthless to bother himself with the effort of stooping to pick up. If he does not finish cigarette #9 in time, he will have no other alternative, when she approaches his desk and asks to borrow a cigarette, than to succumb to her request.

Marvin watches Rhoda (clad in her overcoat and mittens) as she discloses the latest location of the coffee can and filters and spoons the grounds into the machine. He notices that she has left her sack lying limp in a heap like a lifeless animal on her desk.

Rhoda makes the approach to Marvin's office. The sack remains on her desk.

The bus was late, Rhoda says.

Yes, Marvin says. Apparently so.

I didn't have time to buy a pack of cigarettes. Can I have one of yours?

Marvin looks at the unguarded sack. Certainly you may have one of my cigarettes, Marvin says. I'll give you one directly you retrieve some water for the coffee machine.

Indignantly, ungratefully, with obvious disdain and displeasure, Rhoda shuffles back across the office and over to the coffee machine. Before she exits into the hallway, where she will have to walk at least fifty feet to the washroom, she turns and looks back at Marvin.

Marvin is watching her, and having imparted his request upon Rhoda, has taken the occasion to snub out #9 and ignite #10, an act which affords him no little pleasure.

Retrieve some water for the coffee. Sort these documents. Type this memo. Contact the following clients and deliver each this message. Check on this account. Check on that account. Do this. Do that. Who in the hell does he think he is? Treating me like this. Me, Rhoda Gleibenheim, the second-cousin of his immediate superior in the main office. And the wages he pays me? Barely enough to sustain the lowest of living standards.

Such were the musings of Rhoda, Head Secretary of the Branch, as she labored down the hall to perform the task she had been directed to perform.

Marvin Mitkowitz, Branch Manager of the accounting firm, cigarette #10 pinched tightly between his lips, can no longer maintain the superhuman restraint he has employed for nearly a year.

He approaches the unguarded sack.

Rhoda stops before she reaches the washroom and looks back down the hall at the frosted glass door entrance. Why should I do his dirty work? Why should I always be the company mule? Rhoda, the company mule, the company packhorse, the company camel, the company slave. I'm not an executive secretary, I'm an overqualified maid.

Rhoda scrutinizes the washroom door, then wheels about and marches inexorably, indomitably, irreversibly and with a manifest attitude of unbounded dignity, toward the office. She'll have her raise.

Marvin's hand is on the sack.

Rhoda's mitten is on the frosted glass door.

Marvin's hand is trembling in anticipation. For nearly a year he has watched her each day sluggishly, apathetically, yet somehow haughtily enter the office, an act which has given him more than a slight feeling of uneasiness, of revulsion, of intense, almost pathological curiosity. And now, at last, the moment of incident has arrived.

Before opening the sack, he pauses, takes a final long, deep and satisfying drag off cigarette #10.

He snubs the butt with a violent, triumphant stab in Rhoda's ashtray. He plunges his hand into the sack.

Rhoda has waited for this minute much too long. She pauses at the frosted glass door entrance, rehearsing her speech: Mister Mitkowitz, I have endured the severest of working conditions patiently, silently, with the most noble of attitudes, considering the situation. Now, Mister Mitkowitz, I feel it is time that you reward my efforts and talents with an increase in salary.

Rhoda gives the door a firm, decisive shove.

Mister Mitkowitz!

Before Marvin has a chance to examine the contents of the sack, the frosted glass door swings open.

Mister Mitkowitz! Rhoda exclaims.

Marvin Mitkowitz, Branch Manager of the accounting firm, attempts to retract his hand from Rhoda's sack, but finds that he cannot move. It is as if his body has been paralyzed, and only his mind remains operant.

His eyes are round and white like new golf balls, and he looks at Rhoda utterly expressionless.

Mr. Murphy's Wedding

My Life is a Perfect Sphere,
And I Roll From Room to Room

My name is Mr. Murphy, and that is the name of my father and of his father before him. My father's father died today, but my father and I each got married, so I suppose things have a way of evening out, mostly.

I can not trust a woman who is devoted to me and who has been faithful: there is still a chance that she might betray me.

Once a woman has abused my trust, only then can she be trusted. She can be trusted to be untrustworthy.

I trust Wife.

We Were Once Young and Fresh,
But Now We are Old and We Smell

I am a good man…. I am a trustworthy man. As far as I know, I am free of disease. Many of my employers have liked me. I was defeated by only a narrow margin when I ran for Junior Class President of Sparks High School. I have never cheated on Wife. I do not support the oppressors of the underprivileged classes.

I smoke marijuana only when it is appropriate to do so.

I have never enjoyed a pornographic movie.

It is my wedding night. I do not know where Wife is, but surely Wife has found some distraction to occupy herself with in the streets of Reno, the city I have tastefully chosen to be the site of our honeymoon. We have been married nearly four hours now, and though the span of time may seem short to you, dear and sympathetic reader, I assure you that each increment of time is infinitely divisible: between each second, between each tenth of a second, is a mathematically verifiable infinity. You see, I think about these things.

Wife, on the other hand, does not think about these things. As a matter of fact, I believe Wife has a digestive disorder. True, Wife can indeed subdue the effects of liquor, and a liberal helping of marijuana brownies does not seem to make Wife sleepy. Not even psilocybin seems to change Wife's sober contemptuous bliss. Nonetheless, an afternoon of drinking at a wedding reception and a nightcap of a bottle of champagne prompted Wife to turn her head toward me, curl her lips and say: "This tastes like shit."

You see, of course, what I am getting at.

In the Mexican Party of Life, I am the Piñata

Wife's favorite beverage is Almond Flavored Goncourt Bros. Champagne.

Wife does not like to bowl and she does not like to play chess.

Wife's breasts are not small for a woman her age.

Wife does not like poetry, even when I read it aloud, with expression.

Wife has an unpleasant odor which reminds me of licorice.

Wife does not know in which city she was born. "Somewhere in California, I don't know. What's it matter anyway?"

Wife has certainly taken on lovers since we have been married, due mostly to the liberal fashion in which I treat Wife. (You see how good I am to her.)

Wife has no interest in art, literature, philosophy, sports, or anything else that matters in life.

Wife does not like me anymore.

You Can't Steer A Train

My father got married today too.

I attended his wedding.

It was his third wedding. I have attended all three.

I met Wife at my father's third wedding.

My father married my girlfriend.

He married her to get back at me. He wanted to get back at me because of the affair I had with his second wife. My father's second wife was better looking than my girlfriend. Now that my father has married my girlfriend she looks better than she used to. Perhaps this is a temporary affectation. Perhaps she employed the services of a legion of specialists. My father's attempt to provoke me by marrying my girlfriend is not working. I got married today too, and now I have a wife.

My father is not the only one who can get married around here.

My grandfather died today and now he is not married anymore. My grandfather outlived three wives but he did not outlive his latest. My grandfather was a lecher and he was certainly in league with my father against me. My grandfather introduced me to Wife. Wife may have been a daughter of his. Wife may have been one of my grandfather's concubines. All of grandfather's daughters were born somewhere in California, he used to say.

I attended my father's first wedding, though I don't remember the event. I was only two weeks old. I have seen the pictures. I was very small, and I looked like a little white rat, pointy nose and little black eyes that never blinked. My grandfather held me while my father proceeded through the vows at the church and the refreshment line at the reception. I seemed to be always crying, then. My grandfather was teasing me. He was teasing me because I wasn't married.

Twelve hours ago I held my grandfather while my father proceeded through the vows in my apartment and the refreshment line at the ice cooler. My grandfather was teasing me. He was teasing me because I wasn't married.

Before the guests arrived at my apartment I put everything I own into the closets and locked the doors. My family is not trustworthy. They drink too much. They are Irish, and that is why our men are named Mr. Murphy. I am not Irish, though. I believe I am a Turk. My mother was not even sure whose child I am. I suppose this makes me an American. My favorite spirit is absinthe. I smoke fine tobacco, but much too much of it. My father is an anti-smoker. My mother is dead.

The family was not surprised when they entered my empty apartment. They have never seen it any other way. They do not ask me what I do with the furniture and clothes they donate to my poverty. I once told them I give their gifts to worthier causes than myself. You see, I am an educated man and I am an honest man: therefore, I am a poor man.

My father works in a gas station and votes for Republicans.

If I leave cigarettes in the refrigerator, he smokes them.

Psycho-Sexual Responses Necessarily Lead to Cannibalism,
But Just Try to Tell That to Young People

My father's second wife seduced me. I had long hair then. That is how we wore our hair, in those days. She was named Lucy. She had long hair too. She came into my bedroom and asked me if I liked her breasts.

"Do you like my breasts?" she said.

"I have no reason not to," I said.

"You should not read the Bible so much," she said.

"I don't read it that much," I said. "Sometimes I just pretend I'm reading it."

It was then that I knew that she was not trustworthy.

The next morning she pinched my rear. My father was not watching, but I am certain he knew what she did. He has a knack for finding these kinds of things out. I had a slow leak on my left-front tire and I stopped by the gas station after my class that day.

My father looked at me and said, as if nothing at all had happened, "You should probably get an oil change and a lube job while you're here."

That is how I know that he knew.

It's Better to Shoot the Wrong Man
Than Not to Shoot at All

My father's new wife has been undeniably faithful to him ever since she began to be my girlfriend. She was my girlfriend for nine years before she married my father. I was always worthy of her trust.

Now my girlfriend is married to my father, and she has abused me.

She used to beg me to make love to her, "Please," she would say, "Please, I am devoted to you and I have been faithful."

But I am a moral person, and it is, as it will always be, my duty not only to maintain, but to elevate the dignity of my lofty family name.

I do not take the name of Mr. Murphy lightly.

Armageddon: If You Don't Survive, So What? If You Do
Just Think of the Smooth Commute

I met Wife for the first time at my father's wedding reception. She looked out of place because it was obvious she wasn't a Murphy. She was uncharacteristically drunk for a Murphy. By the time she arrived all the beer and wine coolers, except the beer in my grandfather's hand, had been consumed. Murphys can hold their liquor.

My grandfather was propped upright in a beach chair he had brought with him and his gray skin was almost the same color as his gray hair. It is not polite to disrupt weddings in my family. Weddings are sacred and hallowed events. My grandfather was aware of this, so he merely sunk into the beach chair, quietly and politely, and died.

He had just seen the girl who had walked in off the street looking for a free drink. The girl was wearing a Walkman stereo headset and a tight fitting blue silk dress and a nice body. She is the girl I married. She is Wife.

"Ankle straps," he said, and he pointed, and he winked at me. He smiled and finished his beer. My grandfather had always liked ankle straps.

That's probably when he died, though it only looked like he had passed out and sunk into his beach chair. There is no way of being absolutely certain about these things. It is empirically verifiable, however, that the empty can in his hand had been the last beer in the apartment.

The ambulance drivers were trying to get the stretcher down the stairs outside my apartment when Wife first spoke to me. I do not know what she said, but she had a nice voice and she did not have an Irish accent.

The ambulance drivers slipped, and my grandfather's body slid off the stretcher. My grandfather's body landed on its side, and was not badly damaged.

The girl turned to me and said, "I know a way we can get a free bottle of champagne."

"Indeed?"

"If we get married at the Hitching Post," she said, "they give us a bottle free."

"And what is the price of the wedding?"

"Gamble on the Clown of Fortune wheel at Circus Circus," she said. "Ten bucks a pop. Ten thousand jackpot. Free wedding even if you don't hit the jackpot. With the free wedding, free booze."

That is when Wife became my fiancée.

I am convinced Grandfather Murphy would have wanted it that way.

The Winnebago of our Passion is Parked
In a Tow-Away Zone

To the hotel I brought no baggage, excepting Wife and a nearly empty bottle of Almond Flavored Goncourt Brothers' Champagne, compliments of the Hitching Post.

The wedding, also compliments of the Hitching Post, was simple, devoid of ornament, offensive to no person's religion or sexual orientation. An old Negro man, while Wife and I waited our turn at the altar, trotted through the lobby with a partially consumed watermelon balanced in his palms like a juicy pink baby. I did not laugh, nor did I comment to the man concerning the preposterous stereotype he was helping to perpetuate: I am a man who minds only business which is his own.

Already I cannot recall the words of the ceremony, resultant, perhaps, of my reverence for the holiness of consecration, but, more likely, because I was annoyed by the watermelon man's biting and slurping. His name, I learned later, was Berfelle, and he made his living as a gratuity coffer, serving as a Professional Witnesser of Marriages.

When the ceremony was over, I attempted to kiss my new bride, Wife. She shunned me, and said to the Official, "Where's the free booze?"

After obtaining said liquor, Wife, expertly uncorking the bottle and chugging like a sailor, turned to me and proclaimed, with curled lips, "This tastes like shit," puckering her lips and adding, "Lay one on me, baby."

Which I did.

The Official played a videotape he had made of our wedding ceremony, and there, on the wall, were Wife and I, life-sized and slightly blurred on the big screen, myself rather tastefully attired in subdued plaid (the Murphy weave), and Wife displaying her wares in a way which seemed to me inappropriate, for a married woman.

The event was nonetheless surprisingly romantic. I doubt I shall soon forget it, entirely.

Historians Will Speak of Us in the Past Tense

My share of the champagne tossed back by Wife, Wife squatted in the corner of the motor lodge room with her blue silk dress hiked above her thighs and panties, matching blue, around her ankles, Wife not merely squatting but relieving herself vigorously, and with expression, on the carpet, Wife not merely relieving herself on the carpet, vigorously, and with expression, but screaming at me words which sear my ears still, I was relatively certain that no consummation of our union was immediately forthcoming.

"Fuck you," Wife explained.

"I beg your pardon," I said, "but you have your dress hiked above your thighs and your panties, blue to match your dress, around your ankles, the very ankles which may have been Grandfather Murphy's last worldly sight, and, Wife, you are relieving yourself, vigorously, and with expression."

Wife repeated her refrain.

I looked out the window. The moon hung white and slender in the sky like a distant lonely toenail clipping, the emblem of our love.

Usually, when things like this had happened to me, I had played the part of the curious onlooker, the voyeur, for I am a man on whom little is lost. Usually, at times like this, I had found a way to tactfully, unobtrusively, even subtly light a cigarette and pour myself a generous drink, toasting, if you will, the humanity of our idiosyncrasies. This time, however, was different. This time, I had no cigarettes. This time, the bottle was empty.

Failure is Not as Easy as it Seems

Wife's sudden and untimely departure having taken me by surprise, I had the opportunity to consider my position relative to the situation.

Outside my room at Irving's Motor Lodge there were many disturbing noises, sounds which reminded me that I was a married man and Wife had left me. The sounds of police sirens and rubber tires ground on asphalt, the squelches of arming car alarms, a cat on the roof crunching through the loose gravel.

The television in the hotel room did not work.

"Front desk."

"Mr. Murphy in 101. Are there any messages for me?"

"No."

"My television does not work, and Wife has left me."

"It's probably a bad picture tube."

Wife had forgotten to put on her shoes and had been picked up by a truckdriver, or worse.

I drive a 1967 Dodge Polara. It used to be a police car. Now it is my car.

Policemen did not trust me until I cut my hair in 1977. I was twenty then. Now I cut my hair often.

We Can't Help Thinking We Have Forgotten Something: The Tragedy is We Have Not

My position relative to things was as follows:

Approximately 6000 feet altitude.

Second floor, Irving's Motor Lodge.

Facing the West, as had my Irish forebears, looking into a flickering neon aurora borealis.

Fifteen feet from Wife's fluid opinion of me.

Philosophically opposed to all branches of ontology, phenomenology, epistemology, and metaphysics.

On the interstate highway of love, I am roadkill.

I only know what time it is when I don't have to tell somebody else.

Waning tumescence, waxing sobriety.

Four days before the next paycheck from my existentially fulfilling but low paying job.

Consider the sincerity of incompetence.

There are oil slicks in the harbor, but that is preferable to periscopes.

Married and Wifeless.

Being a Murphy, however, has its benefits: Murphies, when confronted with The Great Hopeless, The Ridiculous, and/or The Somewhat Stupid, shave their heads and burrow like moles into the professionally manured soils of adversity.

Bald, I walked down Virginia Avenue, Casinos rising from the earth like flickering Rubik's Cubes, in search of Wife. Hot air pumped in shafts from open glass doors onto the sidewalks, smelling of every person within. From none did I catch the distinct licorice odor of Wife.

In a moment of tender remembrance, of nostalgia, I paused outside the Hitching Post and watched an elderly bejewelled couple commit their wedding kiss and watch their video. Berfelle shared in their toast of Almond Flavored Goncourt Bros. Champagne, and in my imagination, which many have underrated, I too shared the moment with a drink— actually, I believe, lifting my hand to clink an imaginary plastic flue.

Some of Our Colleagues Have Been Incarcerated, Others Have Not
The Point is Moot: We All Do Time

Every woman I have ever met has had a chance of becoming a Mrs. Murphy. All women are assessed with equal consideration and unbiased scrutiny, regardless of weight, shoe size, and melanin level. I have never looked at a woman and not imagined her naked, though I admit to having derived varying degrees of pleasure, or lack thereof, from their respective imagined nakednesses. And though I cannot halt my imaginings from intruding upon the virgin sanctities of pre-blossomed youth, I have never acted upon the advice and recommendation of my healthy testosterone. To be honest, I had hoped tonight, the night of my wedding, would remediate my celibate condition.

At Sparks Junior High School, when I was in the seventh grade, I was propositioned by a girl named Heather McGhetter. Header, as the boys called her, was reputed to spend her afternoons behind the tennis courts, on her knees, ministering to the strained needs of her male classmates. I had never sought the succor of Header McGhetter, not out of fear, but from an apprehension concerning the merits and dismerits of the mysterious and potentially contagious process. The childhood myths about Cooties, I had learned, had become clinically verifiable realities.

In the cafeteria, during nutrition hour, Header McGhetter accosted me.

"Will you meet me behind the tennis courts?"

"Header," I replied, "although I am flattered by your concern for my well-being, and although your weight is counterbalanced by your attractive and ample bosoms, I will not, most certainly not, meet you behind the tennis courts."

"Faggot," said she.

"I beg your pardon?" said I.

"Faggot!" she cried.

Our classmates took note.

Life is a Hair Shirt

I stood on the Virginia Avenue bridge over the Truckee River watching the black waters of time and ice flow like wrinkled cellophane over granite boulders and bottomless sands. I, Mr. Murphy, citizen and registered potential soldier, recalled the significant events of my short life. I recalled my birth, the grinning doctor who spanked me into being, recalled many of my step-brothers and step-sisters and half-brothers and half-sisters and ex-step-brothers and ex-step-sisters and foster brothers and foster sisters and ex-foster brothers and ex-foster sisters and adoptive brothers and adoptive sisters and ex's of both the latter two, recalled the heart-shaped rock I gave to Angela Fisher in the sixth grade as a symbol of my devotion, a symbol which she threw at my head, with precision, recalled knocking for six hours on the door of my prom-date's home before drinking a bottle of whiskey alone on Donner Pass, a location appropriate for my desires at the time, and, as I stood on the Virginia Avenue bridge, I was overwhelmed with tenderness for the world, for its citizenry, for Wife.

I strode toward town with satisfaction, knowing that though I was a Murphy, and though neither Christian nor philosopher, I was, though surely barbarian, no savage.

Imagine my surprise, however, when passing Circus Circus, its glittering carrousel horses and elephants and tigers ringing with jackpot quarters, midget blackjack dealers rocking heavy torsos over unsteady feet, fishnet-stockinged young women spreading elaborately supported cleavage over felt tables—imagine my surprise when, at the Clown of Fortune, I spotted Wife, and not only Wife, but, at her side and tugging the heavy black ball of the machine's arm, an enormous Texan, aglitter with sequined vest and towering Stetson and wearing cowboy boots that sparkled like the heavens. The heavy black ball having been tugged, the four eyeballs of the Clown of Fortune spinning in its head, I saw Wife kiss the Texan. The eyeballs stopped spinning and no jackpot was obtained. From the mouth of the Clown of Fortune issued the familiar coupon, which Wife snatched, for a free wedding at the Hitching Post, and the couple made for the exit, which was for me the entrance, through which I had not entered, and through which they now passed, embracing.

"Wife," I said. "Darling."

She pretended she did not notice me, her lawfully wedded husband.

I knew where they were headed. You see, I was not born yesterday.

At the bar, I drank Old Bushmills, my liquor of choice. A rock and roll orchestra played pleasant tunes from the era before my own, tunes I had heard my parents humming together when they were in love. I did not like the tunes, nor did they elicit fond memories. The singer would not have looked attractive had she been shorn of her vestments. I believe the whiskey was diluted by more than the cubes of ice in my glass. The unattractive singer cast significant looks in my direction.

During the break, she approached, then sat next to, me.

"Buy me a drink, looker?"

"No."

She bore an expression of surprise.

"You got a problem?"

"No."

"Well?"

I smiled, and I thought of my knowledge of love.

"I am Mr. Murphy," I said. "I drink alone."

Skaters

Looking back on it, me and my two younger brothers, Kent and Clyde, were pretty poor when we were kids. We didn't really *feel* poor, though. If we thought we really needed something, we'd just swipe it. One time Kent swiped a pair of Adidas from Oakland Sporting Goods. Clyde copped off with the coolest water bottle for his bike you ever saw. My expertise was baseball cards and cans of raviolis. Pop never asked where we got the stuff, and we never told.

We lived in a nineteen foot trailer next to the Mohawk station where my pop pumped gas, washed windshields, checked oil and fixed flat tires, and we had plenty of fun at that gas station. We'd make gigantic fortresses out of old tires, replete with turrets, towers, and scrap-metal drawbridges. Our tin washbasin moats shimmered with oil and antifreeze.

All year long Pop stashed money in a holiday account, and each Christmas we'd go on a nifty vacation. We camped one year in the snows of Yellowstone. We spelunked in southern Missouri. One year we drove the old highways of the Midwest and swiped signs from abandoned gas stations. We spent a Christmas vacation going to all the missions in

California, and late one night we snuck into the field at Mission San Jose and rolled a wooden wagon wheel back to the pickup, took it back and chained it to the front of our trailer. Eventually we got a deal renting a little apartment on Tahoe Keys, a lagoon-style setup on Lake Tahoe, and that's where we ended up going every Christmas.

It never snowed in Oakland and seldom got cold enough to freeze a puddle. But Lake Tahoe—snow everywhere! And the Keys—they froze over, and so we'd run and slide on the ice. The sky alternated between a sheet of white and crystal blue, and it snowed every other day. Mealtimes we ate hamburgers and hotdogs and cottage cheese, and Pop watched football games on the television. Nights he went to the casinos, and he took us to a play center that was set up for the kids of gaming parents. My brothers and I played pinball and pool and skeetball. Pop took us to see two shows, too: we saw The Osmonds, and we saw The Jackson Five.

Days, though—days we played in the snow and on the ice. We noticed that there were dozens and dozens of kids skating on the ice that wove between the keys, and we went to ask some of the kids if we could use their skates when they weren't using them. They said that the skates weren't theirs, that they'd borrowed them. From who? we wanted to know. From the Admiral.

The Admiral was a very old man, retired. He lived in a small apartment, alone, on the Keys. When we knocked on his door, we heard him shuffling around, and when he opened it, we couldn't believe what we saw: he must have been seven feet tall. He was the tallest human being we'd ever seen. His face was gently wrinkled, and he had a full head of beautiful gray hair, and he smiled.

"Come in, come in," he said. "I'm the Admiral."

We could smell food.

He noticed, and said, "Stew. You boys want some? Take a seat."

He had a banquet sized table in his little front room, twelve chairs arranged around it, places set with plates, bowls, silverware, glasses, napkins. Serving bowls arranged properly on the center of the table, a vase with flowers in the middle.

"You boys skate?"

We nodded. "Yes, sir."

"We'll take care of that in a while," he said. "It's cold out there, and you need some good food in you to keep you warm."

I really wanted to see those skates. What I wanted even more was to have my own pair.

We sat, and he served us what must have been the best beef stew ever made in history. We ate as if we'd never had a meal before. Stew, homemade bread, and lots and lots of butter, which we never got at home because it cost more than margarine. Man, we had butter oozing down our chins.

He went to his fireplace mantle and brought down some pictures.

"My wife," he said, "bless her soul."

She was pretty and young and in black and white. He showed us another picture. "My boys and girls," he said, and there were about a dozen of them flanking the young admiral and his pretty wife, the admiral in full military dress and holding a baby in each arm, another holding on to his leg. "And my boys and girls and their boys and girls," and he showed us another picture and this one had dozens and dozens of people, all of them flanking the admiral. But his wife wasn't in this picture, and the Admiral looked pretty old already, towering over all of them and smiling.

After we ate, we helped him do the dishes and set the table again.

Then he led us to a closet and he opened it and inside were hundreds and hundreds of ice skates, white for girls and black for boys—hockey skates and figure skates and huge skates for grown ups. The blades sparkled and glittered like jewels, like something you were supposed to want but could never have.

He told us to take off our shoes, and then he used a wooden rule to measure our skate size, and then he rummaged around and got us each a pair of skates. He led us outside to the edge of the frozen lagoon, and we sat on a bench while he put our skates on us, showing us the proper way to lace them up. Then he put on his own pair of skates and led us out onto the ice.

"Be careful of ice that isn't white, that's dark," he said. "If it's dark, that means the water beneath is showing through, and that means the ice is thin and you might fall through."

In a single movement the Admiral glided on one skate what seemed to be all the way across Lake Tahoe, his skate glistening in the sunlight, leg outstretched, arms to his sides and sleeves fluttering in a breeze conjured by his movement. He was a young man again.

We stepped out onto the ice, and wobbly-ankled and thrilled we scooted around, cutting tracks in the thin veil of snow from the morning's drop. We were in a world we'd seldom known, a world without the smell of gasoline and solvent and oil, a world without the incessant ringing of the gas station bell, a world where we could move across space without dodging cars and 18-wheelers. We were free and clean and filled with thrill and peace.

Every day we'd skate, and every day the Admiral would feed us, and every day we were not boys from the ghetto who lived on the lot of a gas station in a trailer but boys who skated.

One day, late in the afternoon, the winter sun setting behind the Sierra Nevadas and the clouds in the sky orange and softly burning, Kent was skating far from Clyde and me, and I heard Kent scream and saw him fall through the ice. Clyde started toward Kent, and so did I, but when we got close to him, the ice started to crack beneath us, too, and so we could go no further. Kent's head bobbed and dunked, and each time he came up he was screaming and his face was turning blue with freeze from the icy water.

We heard a door slam against an apartment, and out sprang the Admiral, and he came on toward us from across the lagoon, speed skating with his left arm tucked behind his back and his right pumping across his chest, and we expected him to skid to a stop next to us, but instead he leapt over Clyde and me and splashed down into the ice-hole next to Kent and hoisted Kent into the air.

The Admiral was so tall that he stood on the floor of the lagoon. He walked Kent over to the shore, cracking the ice in front of him like an ice-breaking ship with his arm.

He took Kent inside, and helped him out of his clothes, and went into his bedroom and came back with fresh clothes. He built a fire in his fireplace and made hot chocolate.

It was getting dark already, and we'd drank down our hot chocolate and grubbed all the cookies and cheeseball and crackers we could munch. We put on our sneakers and left.

We'd left our skates outside on the Admiral's porch, as per the Admiral's instructions. After we said goodbye to the Admiral, and he'd shut the door, I circled back to the porch. I stood there looking at those skates. I imagined myself back in Oakland, at a fancy ice skating rink, pretty girls in little dresses swirling and pirouetting and admiring my grace and strength as I flew across the ice, and even though I knew what I was about to do was wrong, I reached down and swiped the skates I'd used, a nice pair of shined and glossy hockey skates, probably the coolest skates in the world. Kent said, "There are some things you shouldn't steal," and I almost put them back, but I just couldn't.

"What if the Admiral is dead next year when we come back? This is what: while the rest of you guys are slipping around on your tennis shoes, *I'll* have skates."

The next year, we came back to Tahoe Keys for another vacation. I'd outgrown the skates I'd stolen, and I needed another pair. I'd felt pretty rotten about stealing skates from the Admiral, especially since I hadn't gotten to use them even once. I was going to figure out how to get the ones I'd stolen back to the Admiral without him knowing I'd stolen them. We went to the Admiral's apartment, and a younger man who looked just like the Admiral answered the door.

We asked for The Admiral.

"The Admiral died this summer past," the man said. "He was my grandfather."

"We're sorry," we said, and we turned to go.

"Wait," the man said. "Did you come for skates?"

We said yes.

"The Admiral, in his will, said any child who comes for skates gets a pair until they're all gone."

"We get to *keep* them?" I said.

"They're all yours," the Admiral's son said.

We went to the closet and got pairs of skates our sizes.

When we were leaving, the Admiral's grandson said, "There's a stipulation, a catch."

"What's that?" I said.

"When you outgrow the skates, you have to give them to a child who doesn't have a pair of skates of his own."

Ten years ago, when I was living in Houston, Texas, an ice-skating rink went belly-up. I went to their bankruptcy sale, bought all their skates. I stashed them in my garage, sorted by size and type.

After Houston, I've lived a lot of places—Santa Cruz, Portland, Seattle, Los Angeles, all over the southwest. Never lived somewhere that froze in the winter.

But now I live in Warrensburg, Missouri. I'm waiting for winter, hoping the ponds freeze over.

I have a debt to pay.

The Teachings of Don B.

I have always preferred not to speak of my ghosts.

Ghosts, however, not only visit me, but disturb my life of love.

I have many books written by dead people. In life, these people were not pleasant. In life, they were drunken sots. Poe, drunk. Hemingway, drunk. Faulkner, Carver—drunk, drunk. Joyce, Stevens, Kerouac, drunks. Now they are dead drunks.

Now they are more dangerous.

I am not a drunk, mostly. I am a good man, mostly. The significant snail that appears to be my liver is, in truth, the consequence of my writerly posture.

The drunken writers, however, were bad men. They were thieves. They preyed on the confidence of young and beautiful women. They were lechers without remorse or regret. In life, they made public spectacles of themselves when they became too happy, and performed unnatural acts when they were sad.

They lay in wait for me to fall asleep, when my girlfriends stay the night.

Then they copulate with my girlfriends. My girlfriends never fail to inform me about this, in great detail, and not without something I cannot help but perceive as pleasure.

My latest girlfriend could only have been described as what we men call a "doozie." Her pubic hair was mowed into a geometrically sound welcome mat, happy sight for many, she once confessed, a weary traveler.

My books are haunted. This does not please me.

We, we professors of English, tell our students that the writers whose works we teach are somehow good people, because they have written good stories and good novels.

They are *not* good people. They are very *bad* people, and should be avoided, especially after they die.

Don B. was my teacher. He died. However, he has not discontinued his tutelage.

On his death bed, I asked him, when he came briefly out of his liquor and nicotine coma, "Don, do you know where you are?"

He said, "I am in the ante-chamber of heaven," he said.

He was Catholic. He had an ante-chamber.

Don B. shamed bad students. He shamed good students, too. Don B's cowboy boots were bigger than ours, and therefore we did not like him. Most estimates concluded that no less than 27 of our apprentice feet would be necessary to fill his left boot, 28 his right, sharkskin. He could outdrink us. Our wives said he could out-copulate us. He wrote better books than we did.

When Don B. died, we were all very happy. He could no longer copulate with our girlfriends, our fiancées, our wives, or the married women we were sleeping with. Don B. was out of the equation. We were very happy students. Don could do things we could not, we had been told.

Don was dead, and now he could not do those things. To our wives. To our women.

Hemingway: double barrel shotgun in the mouth blowing off the back of his head, efficiently. Poe: passed out drunk on the street in Baltimore outside the bar, smoked on his own puke. Faulkner: tried to ride a nag three times and was finally bucked to his death. Carver, Kerouac, and countless others—writer's disease. They were polite and courteous enough not to be Catholic enough to go to purgatory.

Don B. is not polite. He is Catholic. He is taking advantage of his spiritual condition. He lingers in purgatory like a frat boy at last call.

Initially, Don B. was an unhappy ghost. He appeared at a drinking session being conducted between George Blaise and myself. We were both his students. We were his drinking partners. Don B. had copulated with both our wives, George's and mine. They were no longer our wives. Not because of Don B's attentions. Because of the attentions of other writers of less renown.

The first time he schtupped one of my girlfriends, he told her, she told me, "My ghostly phallus is prodigious, if without substance."

"He had this strange white penis," she said. "Rather magnificent, actually."

Don B. came to George Blaise and me of a drinking evening. Don B. was sweating. His nose was purple. He seemed to be crying. George Blaise, like Don B., is Catholic.

"Purgatory," George Blaise said, and lifted a Scotch in toast.

"Unpleasant," I said.

"Most," George Blaise said, "unpleasant."

George Blaise and I were sweating too. Our noses, we knew, were in danger of purpling as we aged.

"My purple nose, like my sweat," Don B. said, "is better than yours. Far better."

When my newest girlfriend, my horticultural doozie, awoke, she was demonstrably and visibly shaken.

"What, my dear," I said, "is the matter."

"I have been schtupped by one of your friends," she said. "One of those writer guys."

This was not the first time this had happened to me.

I shrugged. Someday, soon, I plotted, I too would schtupp one of the women of my writer friends.

"He slapped my fanny and woke me up," she said, "though I may have yet been asleep."

I lowered my eyes, knowingly.

"He said," she said, "'There is nothing to fear. I am a friend of Eric's.'"

My clenched fist betrayed my dislike of feminine confession, to which I have played Father Confessor more times than is tasteful, or pleasant.

"He fondled my breasts," she continued, in earnest sincerity, "most expertly."

"Perhaps," I intoned, "perhaps we should discuss the nagging problem of my spine."

She continued without let or mercy.

"But then," she said, with enthusiasm, "then he unzipped his jeans and revealed his splendor. 'How do you like them?' he asked me. 'Long?' and it was long. 'Fat?' and it was fat. 'Circumcised? au naturale? rippled?

smooth? hooked? symmetrical? ochre, umber, sienna, viridian, cobalt blue, tie-dyed?'"

My girlfriend took my hand, tenderly.

I will not tell you what she decided upon. I have great respect for my girlfriend, as I have for all people of the other sex.

"I can no longer sleep at your home," my girlfriend told me. "Without being unfaithful."

"You could refuse the amorous ploys of Don B.," I said.

"There have been others," she said.

I smiled a smile I have smiled many times before. "But I am your man. You could refuse," I said.

She smiled, and I did not like or appreciate her smile, and she slowly shook her head. "No," she said, and her smile did not wane. "No. No, I could not refuse."

When Don B. was alive, we sat at the bar drinking. I was divorced, and he was schtupping my ex-wife.

"I do not regret schtupping your wife," he said.

"Ex," I said.

"Now," he said.

"She, as well," he said, "has no regrets about the schtupp."

I drank.

"I taught her things from which you doubtless benefited," he said. "Or should have."

I said, "Indeed."

"I will always be a teacher," said Don B.

I had read Don B.'s stories, written under his pseudonym, William W. "How I Schtupped My Student's Woman," and "How to Schtupp

Appropriately," and "Schtupping: a Professor's Guide." I thought I understood them.

Our drink of preference was Scotch, Don B.'s and mine. He was my teacher. My guide through the perils of the nine circles of writerly hell. That was before he began schtupping my girlfriends.

Then he died.

Don B. is dead, and my girlfriend is gone, off to seek more interesting pastures.

I have changed religions.

There is merit in the afterlife.

I do not want to be so bad that I go to hell. Nor do I want to be so good that I strum sheep-guts to the chords of "Pennies from Heaven." I want to spend a significant allotment of eternity in purgatory.

If I go to heaven, though, I want to have a drink with Don B., my professor, a man of refinement in literature, and good taste in women.

Internationally acclaimed novelist and critic Eric Miles Williamson was named by France's *Transfuge* magazine one of the "douze grands écrivains du monde"—one of the twelve great authors of the world. His first novel, *East Bay Grease*, was a PEN/Hemingway finalist, and its sequel, *Welcome to Oakland*, was named the second-best novel of 2009 and one of the top 40 novels of the decade by the *Huffington Post*. Senior Editor of

photo by Judy Marie Williamson

Boulevard, Fiction Editor of *Texas Review*, and Associate Editor of *American Book Review*, Williamson served three terms on the Board of Directors of the National Book Critics Circle. He lives in the Rio Grande Valley.

www.ingramcontent.com/pod-product-compliance
Lightning Source LLC
Chambersburg PA
CBHW050821180626
46814CB00004B/1398